'Thou Shalt Not Suffer....'

by

Tony Green

Cast of Characters with script abbreviations in (CAPITALS). Unless stipulated the sex of the character may be either male or female

The Court

Judge Byron Struthers (JUSTICE) (M)
Ms Gayle DeMarco - appearing for the prosecution. (PROS) (F)
Mr Robin Buell – appearing for the defence (DEF) (M)
Ms Caroline Egan – Clerk of the Court (CLERK) (F)

Witness for the Prosecution

PC Jelkes – Police officer (JELKES)
Mr Peter King – Former Manager at Dunston Assurance (KING) (M)
Doctor Calthrop, MD (CALTH)
Doctor Fisher - Author and lecturer in psychology at the University of Birmingham (FISHER)
Ms Alice Preston – alleged victim (PREST) (F)

Witness for the Defence

Ms Deborah Kay – HR Manager (KAY)
Doctor Foster – Legeesa Practitioner (FOSTER)
Ms Anouska Lacox – defendant (LACOX) (F)

1

The interior of a county Crown Court; in the dock sits a middle aged woman, smartly dressed but for an exotically designed pendant. The councils for the defence and the prosecution sit at desks waiting to present their cases. Before this happens the judge addresses the members of the jury

Scene 1

JUSTICE: Ladies and gentlemen of the jury. The case you will be hearing today concerns an accusation of Aggravated Criminal Harassment against the accused; Ms Anouska Lacox.

On Monday February 18th of last year Ms Alice Preston deliberately injured herself and required hospital treatment. During this time she spoke to police officers and accused Ms Lacox of mounting a deliberate and calculated campaign of harassment against her to such an extent that Ms Preston genuinely believed Ms Lacox intended her specific harm. It was also suggested that she used skills she possessed as a practitioner of the Legeesa religion to help achieve this end and that this was the reason for her wounding herself in an attempt to end her own life. Ms Lacox was interviewed and subsequently arrested and charged with Aggravated Criminal Harassment. She refutes all charges and has pleaded not guilty. Miss Egan, the clerk of the court, will now instruct you further.

(CLERK stands forward)

CLERK: The prosecution and the defence will now present their witnesses. At the end of the case I will speak to you again and ask you for your verdict. You will deliver this by a show of hands against the options of guilty or not-guilty. Thank you for your attention. The case will begin with opening statements from both the crown and those acting for the defence.

(CLERK moves to one side)

PRO: Members of the jury. I would like to make it very clear that, in spite of what you may have read in some of the more…*lurid*…newspapers, Anouska Lacox is *not* a witch. What she is, is a manipulative, clever and malevolent woman who's actions nearly had tragic consequences for her victim. I will present to you evidence that, as a result of an argument at work, Anouska Lacox used the superstitions of Alice Preston, a vulnerable and impressionable woman, along with skills learned through her following of a certain belief system, to torment and harass Ms Preston to the point that she tried to take her own life. It is for this harassment which Anouska Lacox is on trial for here today. Anouska Lacox is *not* a witch – but I think you will soon see that she is perhaps something even more unpleasant.

(PRO sits and DEF stands to address audience)

DEF: Members of the jury. My learned friend is quite right - Anouska Lacox is *not* a witch. Nor however, is she anything else that my learned friend has listed. Anouska Lacox is simply a woman with a certain set of beliefs which the alleged victim – Miss Preston, has twisted in her unhappy and tortured mind. I will demonstrate that Miss Preston is a frightened and vulnerable woman who saw persecution and things to be terrified of all around her. Anouska Lacox, simply by being involved in an ongoing argument with Ms Preston, became the very personification of these fears and the focus of her paranoia. When Ms Preston attempted to take her own life it was not because of any deliberate intimidation on the part of Ms Lacox, but simply because of the general deterioration of her own mental health. A tragic situation but one which Ms Lacox had not part in at all.

(DEF sits)

JUSTICE: Will the Crown please call their first witness.

PRO: I call Police Constable Jelkes

(Offstage – 'Call Constable Jelkes' – Jelkes appears and takes his place in the witness stand. A young but confident police officer who has obviously done this sort of thing before)

JELKES: I swear by almighty god that the evidence I give shall be the truth, the whole truth and nothing but the truth. Number 452, Police Constable Jelkes, Thames Valley Police.

PRO: Constable Jelkes, on February 18th of this year you were despatched to number 23 Ratchmere Drive, Didcot, were you not?

JELKES: That's correct. I was in the area car with PC Lucy Tate. We got the despatch at 07.03. It stated that a woman was injured at the location and in considerable distress. The person who made the call was concerned that she's been attacked so had requested that police and ambulance attend.

PRO: And what time did you arrive at number 23?

JELKES: About 07.10.

PRO: What did you find?

JELKES: A small crowd of people – around six or seven, were in the front garden of number 23. A woman, who I can confirm was Ms Preston, was also in the garden and appeared to be injured in the lower arm. She was wearing a nightdress and it was covered with blood. Someone, I took to be a neighbour, was holding a domestic first aid kit and appeared to be trying to give assistance but Ms Preston was resisting. There was also what appeared to be an overturned refuse bin on the driveway with some household rubbish scattered about.

PRO: What did you do then?

JELKES: PC Tate moved the neighbours back while I approached Ms Preston.

PRO: And what was Ms Preston's demeanour at this time?

JELKES: She was very agitated. She was crying, screaming…She appeared to calm down when she saw that myself and PC Tate had arrived but she was still very upset.

PRO: What happened then?

3

JELKES:	I endeavoured to ascertain the severity of Ms Preston's injuries and find out what had happened.
PRO:	What were her injuries?
JELKES:	She had what appeared to be a stab wound in her lower left forearm. It was deep and bleeding profusely.
PRO:	Was this the only injury?
JELKES:	It was all that I could see.
PRO:	What did you do then?
JELKES:	I was wearing gloves and placed my hand over the wound. I asked Ms Preston to sit down and attempted to elevate it. I also tried to calm her down and talk to her. While this was going on PC Tate had dispersed the group of neighbours and placed a follow up call to the ambulance despatcher.
PRO:	What did Ms Preston say at this time?
JELKES:	Well she was crying, screaming really, if I may refer to my nitebook M'lud? She said: "you've got to help me. Take me to your cells and lock me away. She's coming to get me you see? You have to understand, she's evil and she's coming for me."
PRO:	Did you ask who was coming to 'get' her?
JELKES:	I did, she said "Anouska, she hates me and she's going to kill me."
PRO:	What happened then?
JELKES:	The bleeding seemed to be under control so I asked Ms Preston if she felt able to move into the house. Although the crowd had gone from the garden there were still people about and I wanted Ms Preston to have some privacy. I didn't know who 'Anouska' was and I wanted to listen to Ms Preston without an audience. It was also cold and Ms Preston was only wearing a nightdress. Sitting on the ground as she was probably wasn't the best thing for her.
PRO:	Did she agree?
JELKES:	She did. Together we went inside the house, through a hallway and into the kitchen. PC Tate followed us.
PRO:	Could you briefly describe the kitchen?
JELKES:	It was small, but tidy. There was a small table and chair where I encouraged Ms Preston to sit. I asked her if she had any bandages and she gestured that there was a box in one of the cupboards. PC Tate found them and I bandaged the wound while PC Tate returned to the front door. On the floor of the kitchen I saw more blood and a pair of scissors that also appeared to have blood on them

4

PRO: Did Ms Preston say anything once you got to the kitchen?

JELKES: She had calmed down a little but she kept repeating her accusation that someone called 'Anouska' was coming to get her…to kill her. She also asked to be locked away again.'

PRO: Did you ascertain who 'Anouska' was?

JELKES: Not at this point, I was more concerned with the injury and how it had come about.

PRO: Did Ms Preston tell you?

JELKES: She informed me that she had inflicted the injury to herself with the pair of kitchen scissors.

PRO: Did you ask why?

JELKES: I did. She said 'I couldn't take it anymore…knowing that she's coming. I just couldn't take it.'

PRO: So she had deliberately harmed herself because of her fear of this 'Anouska' person?

JELKES: This is what I was given to believe.

PRO: Did you ask Ms Preston anything else?

JELKES: I asked where she thought 'Anouska' was and why she thought she was coming to get her. This seemed to upset Ms Preston considerably and she once again became very agitated. She said "She's everywhere, she's probably outside watching all of us." She then began sobbing and I decided to not push the point until she had received medical attention.

PRO: At what time did the ambulance arrive?

JELKES: A few minutes later. The paramedics were allowed into the house by PC Tate and got to work treating the injury.

PRO: Did Ms Preston say anything else?

JELKES: She continued to be asked to be locked away. I told her that she needed to go to hospital but that I would see her later and get a statement. I assured her that she would be completely safe in the meantime. Unfortunately this seemed to agitate her again and both the paramedic and myself had to calm her down. After a few minutes she seemed to do so.

PRO: Was this all that was said?

JELKES: No, as she was being helped into the ambulance she called me over and told me that 'everything is in the book' she told me that all I needed to know about 'Anouska' was in this book and she directed me to a drawer in her kitchen where I found an A4 notebook diary.

PRO: At this point we would like to mark this notebook exhibit 1 M'lud

JUSTICE: Very well – exhibit 1.

PRO: Did you read this book, Constable?

JELKES: I did. Once we returned to the station.

PRO: What did it contain?

JELKES: Dates, times, and it listed a number of incidents that allegedly took place between Ms Preston and someone called Anouska Lacox.

PRO: Could you be kind enough to read an example of these? I have printed a copy of the page for February 10th, approximately one week prior to the incident in question.

JELKES: Ok, "Feb 10th, After nothing for 2 days he was only two seats away from me on the bus. I could feel her eyes staring at me. I felt sick. Why is she doing this? I know she won't stop. There's nothing I can say and I'm not even on the team anymore. She's won. What more does she want? I think she wants me dead. Every time I see her she just smiles. A vicious dark eyed smile that I can't seem to get out of my head. I know I'll have nightmares about it tonight. Oh I wish I could sleep but every sound outside makes me jump. I can't go on like this but I don't know where to turn"

PRO: Hmmm, obviously the words of a very concerned woman.

JELKES: That was my thinking.

PRO: After reading this document you went to the hospital and spoke to Ms Preston?

JELKES: The following day, yes. She was much calmer and seemed to be recovering from her injuries. She understood that she would be going home later that day and had booked an appointment to see her GP. However, I told her I had read her diary and that I was concerned about what she had written, and of course, that she had injured herself.

PRO: And what did Ms Preston say?

JELKES: She told me that she had been the victim of harassment by Ms Lacox for some time and that she had written the diary to keep track of it...and to keep it clear in her mind. I asked her what she wanted to do and offered to go and see Ms Lacox. At this Ms Preston became agitated and told me that it wouldn't help. By then I had decided that I would need to speak to Ms Lacox anyway and informed Ms Preston that this is what I would be doing. She eventually seemed to accept this. She said 'I don't suppose it could make things any worse.'

PRO: Now you saw Ms Lacox later that day did you not?

JELKES: Yes, I called her from the station and asked her to come in for a chat.

PRO: And when she arrived what did she say when you spoke to her?

JELKES: Well firstly I asked her if she knew Ms Preston. The moment I did that she rolled her eyes and said 'what is it now?' I explained that I was concerned that the issues between them had led to a potentially serious incident and that I wanted to hear her side. Ms Lacox seemed first irritated and then actually quite angry that she had been asked to discuss the matter. By now

I felt it was wise to caution her, which I did. Ms Lacox then asked for legal advice which was provided and declined to make further comment.

PRO: At what point did you place Ms Lacox under arrest?

JELKES: The following day. I had spoken to Ms Preston at her home that morning and she had agreed to make a complaint of harassment. I called Ms Lacox to the station that evening and arrested her at 19.30.

PRO: Did she say anything after this arrest?

JELKES: Only that 'this is all so bloody ridiculous! If you want to waste your time we can waste as much as you like.' She then answered 'no comment' in all subsequent interviews.

PRO: Well, perhaps we shall hear her side today.

(Ms PRESTON sobs quietly from where she is sitting in the court but composes herself)

Now if we could briefly discuss the injury. Did you speak to the paramedics afterwards about this injury to Ms Preston?

JELKES: Yes, they confirmed that it was a single stab wound consistent with Ms Preston's statement about her using the scissors on herself.

PRO: So Ms Preston injured herself. When you spoke to her did she explain what had finally pressed her to such action?

JELKES: She told me that she had been woken during the night by the sound of her bins being turned over. In the morning she had discovered the bins on her driveway and rubbish on her lawn. She said that it had been the last straw.

PRO: Thank you Constable. No further questions M'lud.

JUSTICE: Mr Buell.

(PROS sits. DEF stands and addresses the witness)

DEF: Constable, was the address in Ratchmere Drive was known to you before the events you have described?

JELKES: Myself and my colleagues have attended the address before.

DEF: In fact the police have attended this address no less than 13 times in the last 12 months is that not correct?

JELKES: I don't have that information to hand.

DEF: Fortunately I do constable. M'lud I would like enter as Exhibit 2 a print of the police despatchers report listing all occasions where police officers had been called to Ms Preston's address between February 2014 and the day in question. Approximately 12 months.

JUSTICE:	Noted Mr Buell.
DEF:	Constable would you look at this report? You will note that you or your colleagues attended Ms Preston's house on 13 occasions since February last year and that you yourself attended in person on at least four of these occasions is that correct?
JELKES:	Yes, by the look of things that would seem to be the case.
DEF:	I have highlighted the occasions when you yourself attended. Would you mind reading them to the jury?
JELKES:	Ok "September 19th – Call from Ms Preston 23 Ratchmere Drive, Didcot complaining of youths outside her house loitering and intimidating her with noise.
DEF:	And the next one please.
JELKES:	Ms Preston 23 Ratchmere Drive, Didcot complaining of a group of youths creating a disturbance at the end of her road. That one was from October 12th.
DEF:	And the next please.
JELKES:	October 30th Call from resident of 23 Ratchmere Drive, Didcot. Resident returned from shopping to find door tampered with and suspects burglary.
DEF:	And the next please.
JELKES:	January 2nd call from Ms Preston 23 Ratchmere Drive, Didcot complaining of possible gunfire in her street.
DEF:	That last one seems serious. Do you recall that specific incident?
JELKES:	I do.
DEF:	Would you tell the court exactly what had taken place?
JELKES:	Well, on attending…well the gunfire turned out to be a neighbour letting off some fireworks he had left over from a New Years party.
DEF:	So no further action was taken?
JELKES:	No
DEF:	In fact in every case on that list where you attended no further action was taken is that not so?
JELKES:	That's right.
DEF:	Not one arrest, caution or even verbal warning is that not so?
JELKES:	That's correct.

DEF:	Would it surprise you to learn that in all other occasions where police attended calls to Ms Preston of 23 Ratchmere Drive, Didcot no further action was taken?
JELKES:	Well…possibly not.
DEF:	Would it be because all the calls were for similar incidents? Noise complaints, accusations of intimidation, people going about their lives in a way Ms Preston found so concerning that she called the police but were in fact, quite innocent?
PROS:	M'lud are these cases really to be considered relevant to the matter in hand?
DEF:	It is the contention of the defence that Ms Preston was prone to over reacting to certain normal events and thus the relevance will become clear.
JUSTICE:	Your objection is noted Ms DeMarco but I am content that the requirements of relevance are satisfied for the moment. Please go on Mr Buell.
DEF:	Obliged M'lud. Constable the noise complaints, accusations of intimidation, in fact every incident that Ms Preston called the police about were in fact, quite innocent were they not?
JELKES:	That doesn't mean that she didn't feel concerned, and we would always encourage the public to…
DEF:	Just answer the question I asked please constable.
JELKES:	I would say they required no further action from the officers responding to the calls.
DEF:	Yes or no please constable. Did they require any action of any kind after the officers had attended?
JELKES:	No
DEF:	So by the very definition of the word they were *innocent* is that not so?
JELKES:	I…suppose so.
DEF:	Thank you constable. I have no further questions M'lud.
JUSTICE:	Thank you constable. You are excused and may leave the stand.

(JELKES leaves the witness stand)

Scene 2

PRO: I call my next witness. Mr Peter King.

(*Offstage* – 'Call Mr Peter King' – *KING appears and takes his place in the witness stand. He is a well-dressed executive with a veneer or professional confidence. As he takes the stand the USHER hands him bible and card*)

KING: I swear by almighty god that the evidence I give shall be the truth, the whole truth and nothing but the truth.

PRO: You are Mr Peter King of Baron's View, Swindon?

KING: I am.

PRO: And would you explain for the jury how you know both the defendant Ms Lacox and the alleged victim, Ms Preston?

KING: I was their line manager at Dunston Assurance in Milton. I ran the product and financial enquiries team and they both worked under me in that team.

PRO: I believe you were with the company for 8 years.

KING: A little over, yes.

PRO: May I ask what your team did at Dunstons.

KING: Mainly answered questions about deliveries, faults with products and issues with billing and invoices. It was effectively a customer services call centre but with a more impressive name.

PRO: And Ms Lacox and Ms Preston worked in this team handling calls and dealing with customers?

KING: That's right.

PRO: It sounds like it might get stressful from time to time, was that the case?

KING: Most definitely. We had targets for everything. Calls answered, time spent on each call, issues resolved, customer satisfaction, sick leave... everything. We had a lot of problems to resolve and often dealt with some very irate callers. So yes, very stressful I would say.

PRO: Ms Lacox and Ms Preston worked within your team under these stressful conditions. When did they join the team?

KING: Ms Lacox had been in the company for over 3 years. Ms Preston for about 18 months.

PRO: Was their relationship good?

KING:	Cordial I would say. When I was there the team consisted of 12 people of a mixture of ages, backgrounds etc. They seemed to have little in common but there were no real issues - at least none that affected their work.
PRO:	When did this change?
KING:	Around October last year.
PRO:	For what reason?
KING:	As far as I understand it Ms Lacox wanted to take some leave, a long weekend I think. However, I was unable to grant it as the team were short-handed.
PRO:	Why was this?
KING:	Two members of the team went sick at very short notice.
PRO:	Was one of them Ms Preston?
KING:	Yes.
PRO:	So Ms Lacox couldn't have her holiday because Ms Preston had gone sick?
KING:	And the other girl. Ms Jenner.
PRO:	Ah yes. Now Ms Jenner was a friend of Ms Lacox was she not?
KING:	I believe so. They used to meet outside of work certainly.
PRO:	And Ms Preston?
KING:	No. She was not one for socialising. She tended to keep to herself. Didn't come to drinks after work if they happened and I don't recall her even coming to the Christmas party.
PRO:	Was she unpopular?
KING:	I wouldn't say that. She just didn't take any interest in the old 'work together - play together' ethos. I'd have liked her to come out more. I think it was good for the team to get together.
PRO:	So Ms Lacox was refused her long weekend because Ms Preston and Ms Jenner were sick. This is what you believe led to the collapse in the cordiality of their relationship?
KING:	I believe Ms Lacox blamed Ms Preston in particular and her attitude towards her seemed to change from that point.
PRO:	In what way did it change?
KING:	Well, the team had a mixture of skills and they tended to help one another as necessary. Ms Lacox was very good with the customer side, even the irate ones. Ms Preston was better at

11

looking into figures and details of invoices. Ms Lacox seemed less keen to support Ms Preston after that.

PRO: For example?

KING: Well, a few days after Ms Lacox had needed the leave Ms Preston had a particularly challenging call. The customer was angry and frustrated - furious actually. Normally Ms Lacox would offer to take the call from Ms Preston but when Ms Preston asked, Ms Lacox just said something like "for goodness sake just deal with it – I'm not wet nursing you anymore!"

PRO: Did you say anything to them?

KING: No, I thought it would all just blow over.

PRO: But it didn't did it?

KING: No.

PRO: In fact the atmosphere within the team became more unpleasant and the bad feeling between Ms Lacox and Ms Preston became ever more clear didn't it?

KING: I didn't notice at first but after a while it became clear, yes.

PRO: Could you describe how things got worse?

KING: Well the first thing I knew was when I received a written complaint about Ms Lacox from Ms Preston. That was about a week after the incident where Ms Lacox snapped at Ms Preston.

PRO: What was the nature of the complaint?

KING: It stated that Ms Lacox was intimidating Ms Preston. Little things really but Ms Preston had found them upsetting. She listed a number of incidents. Ms Lacox took the stapler from her desk and didn't return it. Ms Lacox wouldn't assist her with another difficult caller. There had been some argument about Ms Lacox coming back from lunch late and Ms Preston having to cover her calls. A few small things that Ms Preston felt were making her work difficult and unpleasant.

PRO: What did you do in response to the letter?

KING: Well you must understand, there really wasn't time to do anything. The pressures the whole team were under were huge. We were behind on some of our targets and there really wasn't time to call them all together to sort it out with a big meeting. Once people arrived at work I needed them on the phones. I asked Ms Preston if she wanted to take it further and she said 'no' so that was about it. Once again I hoped it would sort itself out.

PRO: What happened next?

KING: A day or so later Ms Preston was away from her desk for about half an hour. I was told she was in the toilets. I sent Ms Lacox, to see if she was alright.

PRO: And what did Ms Lacox say when she came back?

KING: She said 'Oh shes in there crying again. She does this all the time when she needs sympathy, or *when she's not on sick leave.*'

PRO: Did you ascertain what had upset Ms Preston?

KING: She returned to her desk a few moments later and I asked if she was alright. She said she was so I let it go again. I asked one of the other members of the team, Greame, what had been going on and he said that Ms Preston's plant had died and that she thought Anouska...Ms Lacox, had killed it.

PRO: Did you look into this further?

KING: No, once again we were up against deadlines and targets. I didn't think...well...plant murder...was that important and I had too much to do. You must understand that if you missed your targets at Dunstons – you were gone. The pressure was ridiculous and I really didn't have time to manage my team as I would have wanted.

PRO: Now before we go further I would like to ask what you knew about Ms Lacox personal interests. In particular her interest in Legeesa – spelt, for the benefit of the jury, L.E.G.E.E.S.A. Now, you were aware of this interest were you not?

KING: Oh yes. Anouska...Ms Lacox talked quite openly about it. She brought in books, magazines...even some artefacts - crystals and the like. All the team knew about it. Some would joke with her about it, others seemed genuinely interested. She picked up the nickname 'Sabrina' after a witch in a tv show but she didn't seem to mind.

PRO: What was your impression of Ms Lacox'... shall we say... *interests*?

KING: I didn't really think about it. I mean it was just some faddy thing she was into like palm reading or whatever. From what she told me it was a kind of 'spiritual healing'. The witch stuff was just the team joking around.

PRO: Now one person wasn't joking around was she? Ms Preston was quite concerned wasn't she?

KING: Yes, she took me aside and said that she didn't think it was appropriate in the office and that it made her feel very uncomfortable.

PRO: And what did you do in response to this?

KING: I took Ms Lacox to one side and asked her to keep it, you know, the trinkets and bits, out of site during working hours because it might upset some people.

PRO: You didn't name Ms Preston?

13

KING: No, but from her reaction I think Ms Lacox might have guessed.

PRO: What did she say?

KING: She said 'I suppose that bloody woman has been complaining again. If I could cast a bloody spell on her I would.'

PRO: She said that?

KING: Yes.

PRO: Now it was after this incident that the problems between Ms Preston and Ms Lacox really began to escalate is that right?

KING: I believe so. Ms Preston frequently seemed upset. Ms Lacox barely spoke to her.

PRO: But it didn't stop with the 'silent treatment' did it?

KING: I don't think so. I felt that Ms Lacox was deliberately trying to intimidate Ms Preston.

PRO: In what way?

KING: Well its hard to describe - little things, looks, stares, things like that. On one occasion Ms Preston said she'd found some sort of…well…doll…on her desk. She was very upset and…

PRO: A doll?

KING: Well a kind of…*effigy* I guess. It was just a few bits of straw tied together with a paper clip but as I said, Ms Preston found it very upsetting and it was pretty clear that it was Ms Lacox trying to intimidate her in some way.

DEF: Objection M'lud.

JUSTICE: Yes Mr Buell. Mr King, did you actually see Ms Lacox create this…effigy? Or indeed, place it on Ms Preston's desk?

KING: Well…no…but…

JUSTICE: Then must ask you not to speculate in the answers you give.

KING: I apologise M'lud

JUSTICE: Please continue Ms DeMarco.

PRO: Mr King. Although the details may not have been clear, what was clear is that there was a problem within the team and between Ms Lacox and Ms Preston in particular. Could you tell the court what exactly you did about it?

KING: Well you see Ms Lacox hadn't actually done anything…well…*wrong*. I mean nothing I could discipline her for. I thought the best thing to do would be to try and separate them. A role was coming up in one of the invoicing departments and I suggested Ms Preston might like to consider it.

PRO: And did she?

KING: No, at least I don't think so. When I suggested it she became very emotional. She kept shouting that she...that is - Ms Lacox, had 'won' and 'driven her out of the team'. She was obviously very upset and I felt there was little else I could do. At that point I sought help from the Human Resources Department.

PRO: You made the situation more... *official?*

KING: As I said, I didn't have time to manage the team as I would like. It was incredibly stressful. You were always watching out for this target or that target, always under scrutiny. I let Ms Preston down as a manager I'll admit it...but it was the environment we were working in...the way the whole place operated that was the reason.

PRO: And what did Human Resources do?

KING: I believe they spoke to both of them, or at least planned to. Two days later Ms Preston went on sick leave. She was still off when I left the company.

PRO: No further questions

(DEF stands)

DEF: Mr King is it true that you are no longer employed at Dunston Assurance?

KING: No. I left a few months ago and now work for a company in Reading.

DEF: You left voluntarily?

KING: I did. I had been looking for another job for some time and this one came up.

DEF: In fact you were looking for another job because your team had missed most, if not all of its service targets over the last months of your employment and you had been warned that your employment would be terminated if matters did not improve, is that not so?

KING: Well...yes, as a matter of fact. But the targets were...

DEF: Ah yes, now you mentioned targets earlier. Was one of your targets linked to sick leave within your team?

KING: Yes. We managers were paid a bonus if sick leave was under a certain level.

DEF: Did your team tend to go sick?

KING: Not usually.

DEF: Really? You see I can confirm that Ms Preston had no less than 12 days of sick leave between December 2015 and December 2016. Isn't that rather a lot?

KING: Well... I suppose so.

DEF: In fact its double the industry standard and three times what was required to secure the Dunstons 'Team Attendance Bonus' of a thousand pounds for the victorious manager. Effectively Ms Preston's sickness record was not just a burden to the work of the team but also to you personally wasn't she?

KING: It wasn't like that.

DEF: But your suggestion that Ms Preston moved from the team would have solved a lot of problems wouldn't it?

KING: I don't understand.

DEF: Ms Preston, by your own admission couldn't take the pressure of this 'argument' am I right?

KING: Yes.

DEF: Ms Preston was, in fact, a timid and easily frightened person who always reacted to pressure in a negative way is that not so?

KING: Well I don't know about that.

DEF: No? Were not all the times she went sick during specific times of pressure on the team? Higher volumes of calls? Imminent deadlines? Arguments with her colleagues?

KING: I suppose so.

DEF: You suppose so? I think you *know* so don't you Mr King?

KING: It did... tend to be... when we were busy... or expecting to be.

DEF: She was, in fact, a weak woman wasn't she? A woman who became upset and unwell at almost the slightest provocation is that not so?

KING: Well...

DEF: And the situation got worse because you did nothing! You were an ineffectual manager who only wanted to get rid of a member of your team who was affecting targets. At any point you could have interceded into this silly argument but instead you hoped that the pressure would increase on Ms Preston until she took the option to transfer teams that was suggested to her. Your statistics would improve, your bonus would improve and you could relax. There was no 'campaign of intimidation' was there? There was an argument in a high pressure environment that you thought that by ignoring, a weak link in your team might disappear.

KING: No, not at all.

DEF:	You cant have it both ways Mr King, you either saw a deliberate attempt by Ms Lacox to bully and harass Ms Preston or you didn't.
KING:	It was not like that…I didn't have the time to…
DEF:	You didn't have time to what?
KING:	To…to know what was going on…I mean the team was…
DEF:	Are you now saying that you didn't know *what* was going on?
KING:	Well…I…not entirely…but…
DEF:	So why are you really here? I put it to you that you wanted to use this opportunity to attack your former employer. Every answer you have given seems to involve a complaint about the pressure you were under and the fundamental lack of care that you believe Dunstons had for their employees. You have no real knowledge of the argument between Ms Lacox and Ms Preston because you didn't *care!* You wanted to meet your targets and when you didn't you were encouraged to leave the company. Now you have alternative employment what better way to attack your former employers without any effect on your career? And so here you are!
KING:	No.No that isn't it! If I'd have been given the opportunity to actually manage the team as opposed to worrying about these constant targets I might have…
DEF:	You might have been able to shed a better light on this sad affair. Unfortunately this is not the case. Thank you Mr King. I have no further questions M'lud.
JUSTICE:	You may leave the stand Mr King

(KING, visibly crestfallen, leaves the witness stand)

JUSTICE: Please call your next witness Ms DeMarco.

PRO: I call Doctor Calthrop

(CALTHROP enters court and takes the stand. Calthrop is a well-dressed, middle aged GP. Well-spoken and with a slightly condescending manner. As previously the USHER hands over the card)

CALTHROP: I do solemnly swear and affirm that the evidence I give shall be the truth the whole truth and nothing but the truth.

PRO: You are Doctor Calthrop and you practice medicine at the Procter Road Medical Centre, Didcot?

CALTH: Yes, that's right.

PRO: And you are Ms Preston's doctor?

CALTH: Yes

PRO: And to confirm, you have Ms Preston's consent to discuss her medical situation in court today?

CALTH: That is correct, my duty of professional confidence is not automatically waived by being called to give evidence; therefore, I should not give confidential information without the patient's express consent. Ms Preston has however, given this consent.

JUSTICE: I can confirm that a copy of written consent was provided to the court and is contained within record.

PRO: Obliged M'lud. Dr Calthrop, for how long have you been Ms Preston's GP?

CALTH: About six years

PRO: And how would you describe her health generally?

CALTH: In general terms it was good. She had been treated for depression about 12 months previously.

PRO: Now during 2016 was she on any regular medication?

CALTH: Not regular but I had prescribed her Calufrax and Phospheron

PRO: What are they?

CALTH: Calufrax is a mild mood stabiliser while Phospheron is a tranquilizer which helps sleeping disorders.

PRO: So if Ms Preston's physical health was good why was she on this medication?

CALTH: In around August Ms Preston attended the surgery complaining of increased anxiety and difficulty sleeping. I suggested some simple lifestyle changes may help with this - more exercise that sort of thing. But two weeks later she returned with a similar complaint. Her blood pressure was also a little high so I prescribed the medication for 4 weeks and asked her to see me again after that period.

PRO: Did she give a reason for this feeling of anxiety?

CALTH: No

PRO: So she returned a month later?

CALTH: Yes, she said the medication had been of little effect. Her blood pressure was still on the high side so before any further medication I asked her if there was anything she was particularly concerned about.

PRO: What did she say?

CALTH: She explained about some work pressures and concerns about money.

PRO: So what did you do?

CALTH: I gave her another course of Phospheron to help her sleep and wrote her an employer's note suggesting that she should be absent from work for a week. I hoped that a break from the work stress may improve matters.

PRO: And did it?

CALTH: No, when Ms Preston returned 10 days later she was considerably more agitated and said that she had found it difficult to leave the house. She seemed very worried. I asked her why. At first she declined to tell me but this time I pressed her. I was keen to get to the bottom of things before I suggested further medication or specialist referral.

PRO: So to clarify, she had gone from good physical health to virtual agoraphobia and severe agitation in just a few weeks?

CALTH: So it appeared.

PRO: What did she tell you was bothering her so much?

CALTH: She stated that things at her work were somewhat... *unpleasant.* She felt she was being harassed and her manager was doing nothing about it.

PRO: And you believed her?

CALTH: I'm sure I have no idea. What I *can* say is that the anxiety was very real. All the symptoms were clear, and indeed, concerning. Its something that one comes across a good deal in my profession.

19

PRO:	Would it surprise you to know that the argument with Ms Lacox occurred two weeks after Ms Preston first came to you in distress and by the time you had made your referral the whole matter had escalated considerably?
CALTH:	Not at all. Ms Preston was at first presenting very mild symptoms which became worse in line with what she saw as her work pressures.
PRO:	What did you do then?
CALTH:	At that point I suggested that she should speak to a consultant colleague at the local hospital.
PRO:	Had Ms Preston suffered from such symptoms before?
CALTH:	Yes…a few years before. On that occasion a small course of Phosphoron had seen her through.
PRO:	And on that occasion did Ms Preston explain the reason for her anxiety?
CALTH:	She did.
PRO:	And what was it?
CALTH:	I believe it was linked to the death of a close relative.
PRO:	So it had been a few years since Ms Preston had sought any treatment for this…*anxiety?*
CALTH:	That's right.
PRO:	And when she had previously it was because of a severely traumatic event?
CALTH:	I would say so.
PRO:	But on this occasion her symptoms were worse?
CALTH:	They were more severe certainly.
PRO:	So might we conclude that the cause on this occasion was even more traumatic than bereavement?
CALTH:	Well…
DEF:	M'lud I object. The witness is being asked to speculate on matters significantly beyond his medical expertise.
JUSTICE:	I am inclined to agree Mr Buell. Ms DeMarco would you care to rephrase your question?
PROS:	There's no need M'lud. But I will ask another if I may? Doctor, after the incident on 18 February where she injured herself with scissors Ms Preston was placed under a general 24 hour psychiatric observation at the John Ratcliffe Hospital is that so?

CALTH: That's correct. Its generally the procedure in cases of attempted suicide or significant self harm.

PROS: The psychiatrist attached to the John Radcliffe hospital added his own comments to Ms Preston's medical notes?

CALTH: He did.

PROS: At any point did he suggest that Ms Preton was in any way mentally ill or deranged?

CALTH: No, he stated she was physically exhausted and showing signs of extreme stress but she was *not* delusional at the time he examined her.

PROS: I have no further questions.

(PROS sits and DEF stands)

DEF: Dr Calthrop. To pick up the story so to speak. At the point you referred Ms Preston to your consultant colleague what was your opinion of Ms Preston's condition?

CALTH: I believed she may have been suffering from an acute anxiety disorder. Her symptoms were certainly what one might call warning signs.

DEF: Could you explain to the court exactly what an anxiety disorder is?

CALTH: Anxiety disorders are a category of mental disorders characterized by feelings of anxiety and fear, where anxiety is a worry about future events and fear is a reaction to current events. These feelings may cause physical symptoms, such as a racing heart and shakiness. There are a number of anxiety disorders: including generalized anxiety disorder, a specific phobia, social anxiety disorder, separation anxiety disorder, agoraphobia, and panic disorder among others.

          While each has its own characteristics and symptoms, they all include symptoms of anxiety. Anxiety disorders are partly genetic but may also be due to drug use including alcohol and caffeine, as well as withdrawal from certain drugs. They often occur with other mental disorders, particularly major depressive disorder, bipolar disorder, certain personality disorders, and eating disorders...

DEF: How might they begin?

CALTH: I was getting to that. Anxiety disorders are often severe chronic conditions, which can be present from an early age or begin suddenly after a triggering event. They are prone to flare up at times of high stress and are frequently accompanied by physiological symptoms such as headache, sweating, muscle spasms, tachycardia, palpitations, and hypertension, which in some cases lead to fatigue or exhaustion.

          The prognosis varies on the severity of each case and utilization of treatment for each individual. It is one of the most common causes of workplace absence in this country. It's a potentially very serious condition.

DEF:	So you referred Ms Preston to a specialist?
CALTH:	Yes
DEF:	And this specialist was likely to assess her condition and treat it accordingly?
CALTH:	Yes, once a diagnosis had been confirmed.
DEF:	With medication?
CALTH:	Possibly.
DEF:	With counselling?
CALTH:	Yes possibly.
DEF:	With other forms of specialist treatment which may have helped her condition?
CALTH:	Of course.
DEF:	Had she attended this appointment there may have been any number of possible courses to take to improve her condition isn't that right?
CALTH:	Yes, The condition is very treatable once diagnosed.
DEF:	Without this support her condition may well have deteriorated is that right?
CALTH:	It's certainly possible
DEF:	She may have become paranoid?
CALTH:	Yes
DEF:	Deluded?
PROS:	M'lud are we not taking speculation a little far? As the Defence argued a moment ago M'lud The witness is being asked to speculate on matters significantly beyond his requirement as a GP
DEF:	M'lud I am happy to rephrase the line of questioning.
JUSTICE:	Please do.
DEF:	Doctor, if Ms Preston's condition was indeed psychological would lack of treatment cause her to eventually become more generally afraid and vulnerable?
CALTH:	I think so.
DEF:	Did you feel that it was important for Ms Preston to get this help?

CALTH:	Certainly. I don't waste either the time of my colleagues or my patients by making spurious referrals.
DEF:	But she didn't keep this appointment did she? Or two other subsequent ones you made for her?
CALTH:	No
DEF:	And so got none of the help that may have been offered?
CALTH:	No
DEF:	And so she may well have experienced paranoia and delusional behaviour?
CALTH:	Possibly.
DEF:	Causing her to feel terrified in her own home?
CALTH:	Yes.
DEF:	To…say…call the police at the slightest noise or provocation?
CALTH:	Possibly
DEF:	To see harassment and intimidation from a colleague she was not on good terms with?
CALTH:	Well…Possibly.
DEF:	And all this could have been a result of her condition and not the other way round?
CALTH:	Well…
PROS:	M'lud I must object.
JUSTICE:	Your objection is noted but I would like an answer to the question.
DEF:	Doctor is it possible?
CALTH:	I suppose so.
DEF:	Finally the John Ratcliffe psychiatrist who examined Ms Preston on 18 February, after the incident where she harmed herself. Did he perform a detailed examination?
CALTH:	No, it would be a general observation to ensure she was no longer a danger to herself, that sort of thing.
DEF:	Did he suggest she spoke to a specialist?
CALTH:	He did.
DEF:	To your knowledge Doctor, has she?

CALTH:	Not... to my knowledge. No.
DEF:	I have no further questions.
PROS:	Just before the witness is excused I would like to clarify a point M'lud
JUSTICE:	Very well Ms DeMarco.
PROS:	In your notes prior to this referral you suggest Ms Preston may have been suffering from depression?
CALTH:	Yes
PROS:	You weren't sure?
CALTH:	No, there were other factors which I thought should have been discussed. She seemed easily agitated; I was concerned about her agoraphobia. I felt a more detailed analysis was required before prescribing drugs which may have not worked well with treatments for other conditions.
PROS:	But she had not been diagnosed with any of these 'other conditions' up to January of last year?
CALTH:	No
PROS:	Suppose she had been suffering from depression, that your initial diagnosis was correct. What would be the effect of the harassment you have heard described as being conducted by the accused?
CALTH:	I would expect it would be very damaging to her. The depression would almost certainly become more severe.
PROS:	Severe enough to push her to harm, or even kill herself?
CALTH:	I think so.
PROS:	So Ms Preston was never diagnosed with any psychological condition by any medical professional aside from the possibility of mild depression?
CALTH:	No
PROS:	A condition which would leave one venerable but with full use of their faculties and completely capable of recognising when someone was deliberately attempting to do them harm?
CALTH:	I think so.
PROS:	Thank you Doctor. No further questions.
JUSTICE:	Witness is excused.

24

Scene 4

(CALTH leaves the stand)

PROS: I call Doctor Dennis Fisher.

(FISHER enters and takes the stand. He is a senior academic with tweed jacket, bow tie and round glasses)

FISHER: I do solemnly swear and affirm that the evidence I give shall be the truth, the whole truth and nothing but the truth.

PROS: You are Doctor Dennis Fisher and you work as a lecturer in psychology at the University of Birmingham?

FISHER: That's correct.

PROS: You have also published two books on the subject of what we might call 'the occult' in modern society?

FISHER: I have written two books on the subject of occult beliefs. 'Un-original Sin' and 'If Not the Devil then Who?'

PROS: Now these works take a sceptical view of things like witchcraft, spells and magic is that not so?

FISHER: That would be to generalise. If you ask do I believe in curses, spells and witchcraft then the answer is no. However, my books do not seek to debunk any religious belief, more – to analyse the effect of those preaching religious belief have on those who *do* believe.

PROS: What specifically are the roots of your studies?

FISHER: The theory that with practice, a degree of showmanship, a rudimentary ability in NLP and other skills one can create the idea that one is more than what they actually are. Either as a part of a peer group, on the search for sexual partners, financial gain or even to 'smite' your enemies. My work focusses on the argument that it is possible for a person with these skills to create the veneer of power, confidence, success and even sexual attractiveness by some very effective sleight of hand magic - Particularly in the impressionable. In this way they are able to make people believe virtually anything... that they have mystical powers...

PROS: The ability to curse?

FISHER: Yes, the ability to curse... or simply that they are attractive or their ideas are worth adopting. The charisma of the cult leader is, I feel, very relevant today, particularly in the Western world. We have examples throughout the 20th century... Jim Jones, Charles Manson as the most obvious.

PROS: Now this isn't a new or radical theory is it?

FISHER:	Don't tell my publisher that…but no, mediums and magicians have been doing it for centuries to varying degrees of success. My research covers the effect of such actions on people in society today where education and indeed scepticism are more prevalent. For example – we all know that Derren Brown is not a wizard, my studies focus on to what extent a person with skills such as he might still be able to manipulate people should they wish to do so…and to what ultimate effect.
PROS:	So if I wanted to make someone believe that I was capable of doing them harm, that I was capable of effectively 'cursing' them…how would I go about it?
FISHER:	Well you would need to have certain skills but it would be possible if the person was impressionable. To give you an example – you are a pretty slim person but if somebody, perhaps a friend, said you were putting on weight you might ignore it but it may plant a seed in your mind. If someone else said something similar the same day, perhaps a work colleague, then you might think that you were indeed putting on weight even if you were not. Two seemingly innocent comments from two unconnected people creating a feeling in you that might lead you to change your habits, lifestyle or just start to worry. Similarly, if you believed that you were indeed 'cursed' you might associate any piece of bad luck or ill health you experienced to this curse.
PROS:	To the extent that you might do yourself harm?
FISHER:	Oh yes, never underestimate the impressionability of people. A few years ago two American teenagers tried to kill themselves because they believed they had been compelled to do so by a rock song - an extreme example but none the less compelling.
PROS:	So is it possible to use signals and actions so slight that they build up this image so that it is completely real to the eyes of others.
FISHER:	Of course, if you possessed the skills and the will. And if the person you were 'cursing' was impressionable, gullible or of limited intelligence then the effects could be quite effective.
PROS:	Or if they were of a nervous disposition?
FISHER:	Of course.
PROS:	Now we have heard that the manager of Ms Lacox and Ms Preston believed that Ms Lacox was trying to intimidate Ms Preston in their office but the signs were too small to really act upon. In your opinion could these intimidations - looks, stares, that sort of thing - be used to give the impression that Ms Lacox had 'cursed' Ms Preston, or at least was capable of doing her real harm in some way?
FISHER:	Oh absolutely, but they wouldn't work on their own. There would need to be other elements.
PROS:	Such as?
FISHER:	Well like I said, remarks, possibly the support of others, some accompanying ill fortune…a number of things, both deliberate and incidental, would need to come together…and it would need to be pro-active.

26

PROS:	Like leaving effigies on their desk?
FISHER:	Oh certainly.
PROS:	Like following them home from work?
FISHER:	Yes.
PROS:	Or standing in their garden?
DEF:	Objection. M'lud there has not been any confirmation that these things happened.
JUSTICE:	I agree. If you are intending to present testimony suggesting that these things did actually happen I think that this line of questioning would be best left for then.
PROS:	I understand M'lud, I withdraw the question. Doctor Fisher, you have heard the words of Ms Preston's GP. If she was being deliberately harassed in this manner, would you expect her physical symptoms to progress in the way Dr Calthrop described?
FISHER:	Most certainly.
PROS:	And the subtleties of the actions of Ms Lacox, as described by both her former manager and in the complaints of Ms Preston; are they consistent with such skills being deployed in the way you have explained?
FISHER:	Possibly. But this is why the process is compelling.
PROS:	In this case what is your personal opinion?
FISHER:	I think that the argument, work pressures and testimony of Ms Preston's GP are all consistent with someone being very clever in their manipulations...
	(Ms PRESTON sobs from her seat again but quickly composes herself)
PROS:	Thank you Doctor, I have no more questions.
	(PROS sits and DEF rises)
DEF:	Doctor Fisher, if one had these skills of manipulation and showmanship that you describe to what end would they generally be applied?
FISHER:	Fundamentally for professional, financial or perhaps even sexual gain. Indeed there is an entire culture online that swaps ideas on how one might attract a sexual partner with the use of things like NLP. Others use it to advance in their professional lives, to create a veneer of success or invulnerability to put themselves ahead of their peers and gain promotions, that sort of thing. There are extreme cases of course, cult leaders and what have you, but they are extremely rare.
DEF:	So if such things are possible why don't far larger numbers of people apply these practices or seek to learn them?

FISHER: Ah well that's the thing. It takes a lot of study, hard work and practice. It doesn't come overnight. For most, the 'prize' isn't worth the effort of the application. To use the Derren Brown analogy – he took years to develop his talents and made it his profession, as have some of these people online who discuss the attraction of women. Most people lack the time to subjugate their normal lives to chasing such, pretty unimportant, goals. In fact such commitment to anything in western society is very rare indeed.

DEF: What do you mean?

FISHER: Well... consider the Olympic athlete. They have a talent of course, but they also train from dawn to dusk. They sacrifice their social lives, their family lives, even their own health and happiness in some cases, all to achieve their goals. This is why there are so few elite sportsmen and women. It is the same with the skill of manipulation. This is the level of commitment you generally need to learn and use these skills effectively in this way.

DEF: So let's say that I wished to acquire the skill to terrify someone I didn't like – in exactly the same manner which my client is accused. How long would that take?

FISHER: It's hard to say. There are many factors to consider...

DEF: Weeks?

FISHER: Oh goodness no.

DEF: Months then?

FISHER: I would be more inclined to say years. It requires a good deal of practice, reading, application... Like I said, the reason more don't do it is that the end rarely justifies the effort. To master such skills inside a year would require a considerable commitment of time... I would say, even studied full time, we would be looking at years not weeks or months.

DEF: In your experience, Doctor Fisher, when such people do apply themselves in this way, by this I mean they study for years to develop these skills, what are their motivations?

FISHER: They are usually after a pretty big reward. One tends to find such people have considerable aspirations towards personal success. They are willing to commit all their personal, and in some cases, their professional lives, to achieving their goals.

DEF: Fortune, fame and glory?

FISHER: Exactly

DEF: Not working in a trading estate call centre?

FISHER: Not at all.

DEF: Or harassing their work colleagues?

FISHER: Not in isolation, no.

DEF: I have no further questions.

JUSTICE: Witness is excused.

             (FISHER leaves the stand)

Scene 5

PROS: I call Ms Alice Preston

               (PREST takes to the witness stand. She nervously looks at the defendant and regularly takes
               a deep breath before speaking. She is either of fragile demeanour but extreme courage, or
               she is ill and barely able to contain her fears)

PREST: I swear by almighty God that the evidence I give shall be the truth, the whole truth and
               nothing but the truth.

PROS: You are Ms Alice Preston of 23 Ratchmere Drive, Didcot?

PREST: I am.

PROS: Do you need a glass of water?

PREST: No, I'm all right.

PROS: Very well, if you do please let me know and I'll pause for a moment.

PREST: Thanks

PROS: No if we could begin I'd like to ask you about your relationship with Ms Lacox. You have
               been working at Dunstons for quite a while. How was your relationship at first?

PREST: I suppose we had a good relationship. I was quite good at the accounting side of things. I
               could go through a customer's record and see any problems with the account pretty quickly.
               I wasn't so good with people who were angry or didn't want to listen to any explanation.
               Anouska was very good at calming people down or simply getting them to be quiet long
               enough for us to get to the bottom of the problem. Sometimes people just wanted someone to
               shout at... I wasn't so good at those sort of calls. Anouska tended to call me over if she
               couldn't see where a billing problem was or something like that. I tended to call her if the
               customer was... well... irate.

PROS: So you were friends?

PREST: No, I mean we liked different things. Anouska liked to socialise, go to the pub, the gym that
               sort of thing. I preferred staying in so we had very little in common but we never argued if
               that's what you mean. The whole team was nice really.

PROS: But this changed?

PREST: Yes

PROS: Around when?

PREST: The weekend of the first of October. I was quite unwell. I couldn't work Friday or Saturday
               morning as I was on the rota to do. I know it was inconvenient but I really couldn't work. I
               could barely get out of bed. I was better by the Monday but when I got in Anouska seemed

very angry with me. I didn't know she had been called in, or that she had plans for that weekend that had been spoiled until later. If I had known I'd have apologised to her but instead I just came in and got on with things.

PROS: When did you notice a change in Ms Lacox attitude towards you?

PREST: Someone else on the team asked me if I was feeling better and I said that I was. Anouska sort of 'tutted' and rolled her eyes. I asked her if anything was the matter and she said something like 'oh no – everything's just fine!'

PROS: In an aggressive way?

PREST: No, more sarcastic really. I decided to pay it no mind.

PROS: But things got worse?

PREST: Slowly yes. Over the next couple of days there were... little things. Like if Anouska was making a coffee she asked the people near her if they wanted one but not me. In the past she's always got coffee for everyone you see? Then as I was coming in one morning she didn't hold the lift... that sort of thing... little... I suppose you'd call them... *slights*. At least at first.

PROS: Did you speak to Ms Lacox about this?

PREST   Well, no, not really. I did ask Hannah, another girl on the team, what was up with her though.

PROS: What did she say?

PREST :   She told me about Anouska having to work the weekend and that she had missed something important. She said she wasn't happy about it.

PROS: Did you approach Ms Lacox once you knew the problem?

PREST: No, I mean... well I wasn't the only one off who was supposed to have been in that weekend and... well... I didn't see why I should apologise for being Ill. Mr King was the one who had asked her to come in so it wasn't really my fault. I just thought it would all blow over.

PROS: But it didn't?

PREST: No. If anything the hostility became more obvious. The... comments were... just little snipes really. You got used to them. I just wanted to get on with my job. The work was pretty involved so it was easy to just get on with things. Then there was the problem with the customer on the phone.

PROS: What happened with that?

PREST: I took a call from a customer I'd had trouble with before. He was a pretty big customer and a delivery he had been expecting hadn't arrived. I was trying to make sense of the tracking screen and he just kept shouting. Anouska...Ms Lacox...had spoken to him before and I tried to get her attention to ask for some help.

PROS: What did she do?

PREST: At first she ignored me. Then, when I finally got her attention and explained the problem she snapped back something like...'I'm not helping you anymore'...or something like that.

PROS: Mr King suggested it was more like 'I'm not wet-nursing you anymore.'

PREST: Yes, that's it. That was the first time that I realised that it wasn't going to blow over. We had always worked hard for the customers but this...what she said was...

PROS: It was then that you decided to speak to your manager, Mr King?

PREST: I was worried I'd do something silly like burst into tears or something so I wrote a letter. It was the best way to gather my thoughts. I explained about the looks, the...slights and how I was beginning to feel that it was personal and that the job I enjoyed was becoming difficult...unpleasant.

PROS: And what did Mr King do?

PREST: Well he was very busy. He asked if I wanted to get HR involved and it all seemed a bit unnecessary. I was just hoping he'd speak to Anouska and to get her to stop but he was going to make it all official so I told him to forget it.

PROS: What happened next?

PREST: I think it was the following day. I came to see that my...well this is going to seem very silly...my spider plant had died.

PROS: This was a plant you kept on your desk?

PREST: Yes, it was my mothers. She died a couple of years ago. That was why the plant was special you see? She...my mother...she was a very keen gardener...when she died we had to sell the bungalow...the plant was one of the only things I kept of hers...it was like a part of her was still...

PROS: Do you need a moment?

PREST: No...(*Composes herself with a sharp breath*) I came into work and it was dead. This was a Monday. It was fine on the Friday.

PROS: You suspected it had been deliberately tampered with?

PREST: Spider plants don't just die in two days. They're very hardy. Something must have been done to it. Salt water or some other poison...I just couldn't take it...I burst into tears and had to go to the toilets to collect myself. I mean I couldn't believe that someone would...*do* something like that.

PROS:	And you're convinced it was Ms Lacox?
PREST:	I was on good terms with everyone else...who else could it be? I assumed she'd heard about my letter to Mr King and...
PROS:	And he spoke to you?
PREST:	Not this time, but he spoke to Anouska I think.
PROS:	And did matters improve?
PREST:	No. They got worse.
PROS:	In what way?
PREST:	Well I'd known for a while that Anouska had been interested in...well...some sort of exotic religion...she had talked about it to some of the team and they'd given her a nickname after a witch in a television show.
PROS:	What did you think of that?
PREST:	Well...I didn't think it was particularly appropriate for the workplace but...well it was none of my business really...Then I started to notice Anouska staring at me...just every now and then across the desk...and she's mutter to herself...Once I asked her what she wanted and she said nothing...one of the team...Jenna...said something like..'oooh watch out! She's cursing you!' or something. The rest of the team laughed...so did Anouska...but there was something in the way she looked at me...something...it was like there were...*monsters* behind her eyes...Could I...could I have some water please?

(CLERK fetches a carafe and glass)

PROS:	You felt uncomfortable?
PREST:	No...I felt...frightened.
PROS:	And you spoke to Mr King?
PREST:	Yes, he spoke to her again...the following day there was a...*thing*...on my desk when I arrived at work.
PROS:	I would like to mark this Exhibit 3 M'lud. It is the...effigy...Ms Preston found on her desk.

(PROS holds up a mixture of twigs and leaves roughly twisted into a human shape and held together with string and paperclips.)

JUSTICE:	Very well, Exhibit 3.

(LACOX shakes her head from the dock)

PROS:	What happened then Ms Preston?

PREST: I felt physically sick. I didn't know what it meant but I...I...I don't know how I got through the day...Its all a bit of a blur...Its like I was in a...a...daze...the next thing I remember was being on the bus...and she was there.

PROS: On the bus you mean?

PREST: Yes, a few seats away from me. She never took the bus...not ever...she had a car and lived in the opposite direction. I couldn't think what she was doing there...and then...then she turned to look at me...and there they were again...the monsters...the monsters behind her eyes...staring at me...and I couldn't...I couldn't look away

(light in court begins to flicker. Some look at the light – at this point it isn't clear if this is a staged error or legitimate part of the play)

...and they were so *dark* ...black like emeralds...like...like they are now...look! You can see...the way she's looking at me now it's the same, its *exactly* the same! Oh my God! OH MY GOD!

(Lights suddenly all go out. Preston screams and begins to hysterically sob)

JUSTICE: It seems that there has been a small technical issue. I will adjourn the court for 20 minutes while we hopefully solve matters. Please be back here in 20 minutes.

CLERK: If you would like to follow me and my colleagues refreshments are available in the long gallery.

(Audience file out guided by front of house team dressed smartly as ushers)

END OF ACT 1

Scene 1

(Court is ready to re-commence. PRESTON is on the stand)

JUSTICE: Ladies and Gentlemen of the jury I trust you are suitably refreshed. The court offers its apologies. It seems a technical issue beyond our control led to a problem with the electrical system in the lighting. I am informed that the matter has been resolved and I thank you for your patience. Ms DeMarco I am aware that Ms Preston was considerably distressed when we lost the lights. I trust she is calmer now?

PROS: She is M'lud.

JUSTICE: Very well then, if you would like to resume your examination of this witness?

PROS: Thank you M'lud. Ms Preston. If you could return your mind to this bus journey. Now please, take your time…you said that Ms Lacox was sitting there on the bus staring at you?

PREST: Yes.

PROS: And that because of where she lived she had no business being on the bus at all?

PREST: Yes, a few seats away from me. Like I said She never took the bus…not ever…she had a car. She also lived in the opposite direction. She lived in Wantage and the bus…the 4C…goes nowhere near there.

PROS: Did she say anything to you?

PREST: No…she just…stared at me. All the way to Didcot…I couldn't wait to get off the bus…I felt sick…I just wanted to get away from her.

PROS: You got off at your normal stop?

PREST: Yes, I got off and I ran…I ran home.

PROS: What did you do then?

PREST: Locked the door and closed the curtains. I was just so frightened. I tried to write everything down…everything that had been going on…so that it was clear…I tried to get it all down.

PROS: By this time you had been given some medication by Doctor Calthrop to help you remain calm and relax. Did you take any on this occasion?

PREST: No

PROS: Why not?

PREST: Because I wanted my head clear. I wanted to be able to recall everything that was going on. I wanted to write clearly what Anouska was trying to do…I couldn't do that if I was drowsy with pills. Anouska was clever... she was... well... I needed to be clever too so I just wrote everything down... every detail.

PROS: Now in your diary you say that nothing further happened for two days is that right?

PREST: Its true... but I had called in sick to work... I couldn't face... well... I couldn't face her looking at me. I just stayed at home. I tried to get some sleep but I couldn't. I went to see Dr Calthrop again but he just gave me more pills and advised me to exercise. Eventually I just had to get on with things so... I went back to work on the Wednesday.

PROS: And what was it like at work?

PREST: The same as usual... the odd look, the silences.

PROS: Was Ms Lacox on the bus when you left?

PREST: I ordered a taxi... I couldn't face the bus... not straight away.

PROS: And the next few days? What were they like at work?

PREST: The same... the odd look, the silences. Sometimes I would catch Anouska staring at me out of the corner of my eye. I just took a deep breath and tried to... well... ignore it I suppose. I mean it was getting so that I was terrified to go out of my own house... it was... well it was ridiculous... I didn't deserve it... but it was beating me.

PROS: Now if we could move to events of the 16th. Some four days after you returned to work. It notes in your diary an incident that night, that is Monday the 16th. If you could, and in your own words, could you describe it for the court?

PREST: Yes... well... It was on the Sunday night, I hadn't been sleeping well over the previous few days but that night I'd been able to get off somehow. It must have been about half past three when I woke up. I don't know what made me wake up then but I'm sure of the time because I looked at my clock radio. I had to work in the morning you see and I was concerned that if I didn't get back to sleep I'd be exhausted the following day. Anyway, I got out of bed and went to the window and there she was, Anouska standing in my front garden just... *looking* at the house.

PROS: You're certain it was her?

PREST: Oh I'm certain... I saw her quite clearly and she was just... looking. Standing perfectly still and... looking. And it was her eyes... her *eyes!* I'd never seen her looking like that before. So intense, like a cat getting ready to pounce. I couldn't look away and she just kept staring...

PROS: For how long?

PREST: I don't know... I don't know. Eventually I just pulled the curtains shut and... oh I know it sounds stupid but I hid under the covers... like a child I hid under the covers of my bed. I was listening for the slightest noise in the house... or the doors opening... when it was morning I could barely open the curtains... I still expected to see her there...

36

PROS: What did you do then?

PREST: You must understand... I was so frightened... it was like I was going to explode... I hadn't slept properly for days... so... I tried one of Dr Calthrop's wretched pills. I didn't know what it would do to me so I... I called in sick to work and well... I just tried to get to sleep. I knew if Anouska was working she wouldn't be outside so I felt... well... fee.

PROS: And did you manage to sleep?

PREST: Yes, for a while... until I was woken up by...

PROS: By what Ms Preston?

PREST: By someone banging on my front door.

PROS: Banging? Not ringing the doorbell?

PREST: No, it was like someone was punching it - half a dozen times. I got up and went to the door but... but there was no-one there.

PROS: And what time was this?

PREST: Around Six thirty in the evening.

PROS: Did this happen again?

PREST: The same time the following evening. Six Thirty. I had stayed home from work again but this time I hadn't taken any of the pills. I just... sat in the living room with the curtains closed. It was like I was just... waiting... and then the banging on the door... bang... bang... bang... bang... like the shots from a gun... but harsher somehow...

PROS: And did you answer the door on this occasion?

PREST: (strangely calm and distant) No... I knew it was just Anouska... and she wouldn't be there if I opened the door...

PROS: So now we come to the incident of the 18th. Can you tell the court what happened that morning?

PREST: I hadn't slept again... although I had dosed a little... five or ten minutes... no more than that really... about half past six... maybe a quarter to seven there was a bang outside... a loud noise that started me awake... after a few minutes I looked out of my window and saw that there was rubbish all over the garden... the dust bin was on its side and... there was rubbish strewn all about... and... (fighting for control over the urge to completely cave in and weep)..and I just knew... I just knew..it was her and she was coming... and I couldn't wait any longer... I couldn't just sit there and...wait... the next thing I knew I was in the kitchen and I saw the scissors... they were on the work surface... strange... they were the only thing on the work surface... and there it was... the answer... just lying there on the side... I don't really remember what happened next. I remember the pain... it was far worse than I imagined... and crying out and... then I was outside... on the doorstep and there were people everywhere...looking at me...and I knew that it hadn't worked...and she was still coming...and she'd *always* be coming...

PROS: Ms Preston, I have just one more question and it is very important that you are clear for the court. When you injured yourself with the scissors what was the reason?

PREST: Because I couldn't stand it anymore...I couldn't stand waiting for whatever Anouska was going to do next...It was the only control I had left. I knew that it would...it would at last...*stop*. No more waiting for the banging on the door, for the looks at work with those...black, terrifying eyes...and whatever she was building up to by following me home...and...being there in the middle of the night...it wouldn't happen if I could just...just...make it all stop.

PROS: Thank you Ms Preston. I have no further questions.

(PROS sits DEF stands)

DEF: Ms Preston before we talk about your relationship with Ms Lacox I would like for a moment to discuss your general health if I may. In particular the bout of sickness that led to you being absent from work on the first weekend of October. In fact the one which you said caused the...bad feeling...between yourself and Ms Lacox. Now I wonder if you could tell the court what the nature of this illness was?

PREST: It was...well...a mixture of things really.

DEF: Could you be more specific please?

PREST: I had a severe headache which also caused me to vomit a few times. It came on on Thursday night and didn't really settle down until Sunday. I couldn't eat or sleep and painkillers didn't seem to do anything. It was dreadful.

DEF: Had you suffered from these headaches before?

PREST: On occasion, yes.

DEF: Had you sought medical advice?

PREST: Yes, well...I think my doctor thought it was linked to blood pressure. He advised me to take more exercise, stop eating salt, that sort of thing.

DEF: And did you do any of these things?

PREST: I tried to take more walks...

DEF: Indeed. Now after your sickness in early October you state that this is when relations between yourself and Ms Lacox deteriorated and this...*harassment* began. I'd like to look at some of the specifics of this alleged harassment if I may.

(Picks up copies of notes from Preston's book)

Now you state a number of accusations such as not offering to make coffee, not holding a door open, that sort of thing. Would you say that you felt harassed on each of these occasions?

PREST: Well...I don't know...at first I just assumed she was in a bad mood and that it would all blow over.

DEF: I see...now Ms Preston may I ask – at what point did you actually begin to feel *harassed* by Ms Lacox?

PREST: It's not...It wasn't like that...it wasn't one thing...it wasn't a particular point. It was...like a steady progression of things, one after the other.

DEF: A great many things by the look of things Ms Preston. Indeed, I have a copy of the pages from your...*harassment* diary here. Would you tell the court Ms Preston, exactly how many specific instances of harassment that you directly blame on Ms Lacox you have noted in this document?

PREST: Well...I...I don't know...exactly.

DEF: I'll tell you Ms Preston – From when you first began keeping the diary in November to the incident of 18th February you list over 200 instances; approximately four a day, every day you worked for just under three months - looks, comments, slights...lack of offers of... coffee. In fact this document begins to read as something of an obsession in of itself...

PROS: *(Stands)* Objection M'lud

JUSTICE: Agreed Ms DeMarco. Mr Buell I must ask you to moderate your tone and kindly ask your question if you have one.

DEF: I apologise M'lud. Ms Preston. Are you completely sure that every note you have made in this document in reference to Ms Lacox is an example of her harassing you?

PREST: I...well...don't you *see?* That's how she did it. Sometimes it was just a look...barely anything...other times it was more...*deliberate.* I wrote everything down because you could never be sure...because only by writing it all down could anyone see...could anyone understand.

DEF: I think the court is beginning to understand Ms Preston. Now moving forward I'd like to look at some of the more serious accusations you make – some of the more *deliberate* examples. Lets begin with the...what shall we call it? The *effigy* you found on your desk. Did you see Ms Lacox create this effigy?

PREST: No

DEF: Did you see her produce it from a bag or a desk drawer for example?

PREST: No

DEF: Did you hear Ms Lacox discuss the item with colleagues?

PREST:	No
DEF:	Did you see Ms Lacox place the item on your desk?
PREST:	Well… no.
DEF:	In fact, is there anything whatsoever that would suggest that Ms Lacox was in any way involved in this incident?
PREST:	No… but…
DEF:	In fact is it not possible that someone else in the team placed this… item?
PREST:	I suppose its possible.
DEF:	I wonder how possible it is that Ms Lacox is innocent of any number of these instances you have listed Ms Preston. Now moving on to the incident of February 10th. You say that Ms Lacox deliberately got on the same bus you did and followed you home from work?
PREST:	Yes
DEF:	The bus, the 4C, leaves Milton trading estate and goes through Didcot is that right?
PREST:	Yes
DEF:	How far from your road does it stop?
PREST:	Just at the bottom
DEF:	Can you see your house from the bus stop?
PREST:	No, the road curves you see? Its only about 100 meters from it though.
DEF:	Now I'd like you to think very carefully Ms Preston. Did Ms Lacox get off the bus at your stop?
PREST:	Well… No
DEF:	You also said it went nowhere near where Ms Lacox lived in Wantage. Did you know that the 4C in fact does go to Wantage, albeit by a slightly convoluted route?
PREST:	I didn't….but…
DEF:	Now moving on to the most harrowing incident of those listed… the appearance of Ms Lacox on your property in the middle of the night. Now you say that on February 16th you were woken at three thirty in the morning?
PREST:	Yes.
DEF:	But you don't know how or why?

PREST:	No…I suppose…no not really.
DEF:	And you went straight to the window?
PREST:	Yes.
DEF:	You didn't put on a dressing gown or anything like that?
PREST:	No, the house was quite warm and I wore…pyjamas that night so it wasn't immodest.
DEF:	And when you got to the window you saw Ms Lacox?
PREST:	Yes.
DEF:	Were there any cars parked in the road outside your house?
PREST:	No. The street was very quiet. Most cars are parked on driveways anyway and I don't drive myself so…no
DEF:	You're sure…Definitely no cars at all outside your house?
PREST:	No.
DEF:	Now you say you saw Ms Lacox' face?
PREST:	Yes
DEF:	Quite clearly?
PREST:	Yes
DEF:	She wasn't wearing a hat or a hood that obscured her features?
PREST:	No
DEF:	What *was* she wearing?
PREST:	What?
DEF:	What was Ms Lacox wearing?
PREST:	I…I can't really remember.
DEF:	You did see her clearly?
PREST:	Yes
DEF:	Was she wearing a coat perhaps?
PREST:	I'm not sure.

41

DEF: Was she carrying anything?

PREST: No, I do remember that. She was standing there with her hands by her side. She had nothing in them.

DEF: Not an umbrella or anything like that?

PREST: No...

DEF: You see I'm a little surprised by this. On the night of 16ᵗʰ February there was one of the fiercest thunderstorms of the winter. It rained solidly from 9 in the evening to around 5am the following day with no let up. It was in the news - Didcot railway station was flooded and roads were blocked causing transport delays. The Thames burst its banks in both Culham and Botley. It was quite a storm...

          So you see I was just wondering why Ms Lacox, who had taken the time to come across town to stare at your house in this dreadful downpour, hadn't brought an umbrella, wasn't wearing a hood or even a hat.

PREST: I...I...

DEF: I'm also wondering why you can remember perfectly what *you* wore that night but don't seem to be able to remember what Ms Lacox, this terrifying, demonic figure tormenting you was wearing at all.

PREST: But it was...

DEF: Furthermore I'm wondering how she came to be there if she hadn't parked her car outside your house?

PREST: Well...she may have parked it further up the street.

DEF: And walked?

PREST: Yes

DEF: And without a coat or umbrella got drenched doing so?

PREST: Well I...

DEF: Finally, Ms Preston, I'm wondering why you can't even remember the storm. You stood by your window, you looked out at the street, you remembered the lack of cars and the details of my client's face but that is where your recollection ends. I find that very odd. Can you shed any light whatsoever on these mysteries Ms Preston?

PREST: I...No...but it WAS Anouska! It WAS!

DEF: I wonder if you were tired and dreamt it. You said you hadn't been sleeping properly. Is that possible?

PREST: I know what I saw. You're trying to twist things...make nasty little insinuations that might suggest that I'm crazy or paranoid or...or just some lonely spinster looking for a little attention by being melodramatic...but that's NOT how it as. What Anouska did was as real as this courtroom...as real as you and Ms DeMarco...as real as the wood on the walls, or the faces of the jury or even those BLOODY BLACK EYES she's looking at me with now!

JUSTICE: Ms Preston I must ask you to moderate your language while in this courtroom.

PREST: I...I'm sorry M'lud.

JUSTICE: Accepted. Mr Buell, do you have any further questions?

DEF: I have no further questions M'lud

JUSTICE: The witness is excused.

            (PREST shakily leaves the stand and returns to her seat)

PROS: With this witness the prosecution rests.

JUSTICE: Very well, Mr Buell will you call your first witness?

DEF: I call Ms Deborah Kay.

(KAY enters the witness stand. A well-dressed professional with a confident air.)

KAY: I swear by almighty God that the evidence I give shall be the truth, the whole truth, and nothing but the truth.

DEF: You are Ms Deborah Kay and you worked at Dunstons Assurance in the Human Resources Department?

KAY: That's right, I have worked as an HR consultant for 12 years. For the last 5 at Dunstons

DEF: Now we have heard that there was an argument between Ms Preston and Ms Lacox in October of last year, and that while Mr King, her team leader and immediate superior, tried to deal with it, albeit ineffectively, eventually the Human Resources Department were informed. Could you tell us what happened then?

KAY: About the first week of February I was approached by Mr King and asked for advice about a situation which appeared to have developed within his team. Mr King was concerned that the atmosphere between Ms Lacox and Ms Preston was affecting the work of both themselves and the rest of the team. He wanted some advice as to how to proceed.

DEF: If it's a simple 'atmosphere' as you put it, would a manager really be expected to bother Human Recourses as opposed to dealing with it themselves?

KAY: No, not normally but he was concerned about the religious element, things like that generally need to be handled carefully, and the fragility of Ms Preston

DEF: Fragility?

KAY: Yes, I believe Mr King's words were 'she tends to fly off the handle' or something to that effect. I got the feeling that he wanted some professional phrases he could use to effectively bang their heads together.

DEF: Now this was not the first time you had heard Ms Preston's name was it?

KAY: No. I had completed paperwork regarding her levels of sickness absence over the last year just a few days previously.

DEF: To what end?

KAY: Ms Preston was to receive a written warning regarding her attendance at work.

DEF: Had you had any personal contact with Ms Preston herself up to this point?

KAY: Yes, a few weeks previously she had made a complaint of harassment against a member of her team who she declined to name. Instead she passed me her diary and asked me to read it. She said she wouldn't name the colleague.

DEF:	Did you ask her why?
KAY:	No, I took the diary and read it as she asked. Her request wasn't unreasonable. Accusations of this nature can be very serious and people tend to be hesitant about making them. I also got the impression that she wanted to see if what she had noted in her diary did, in fact, constitute harassment in the workplace.
DEF:	And did it?
KAY:	Well it's hard to say. The document placed a lot of emphasis on what I would call a 'lack of courtesy' as opposed to specific targeted bullying. I suppose I was looking for evidence that there had been any actual harassment in the terms which the business and its policies would define it. Effectively conduct which has the purpose or effect of violating an individual's dignity or creating and intimidating, hostile, degrading, humiliating or offensive environment for that individual. While Ms Preston's apparent reaction to some of the instances she placed in her diary was one of feeling intimidated, in was very difficult to see how it could have been deliberate.
DEF:	For example?
KAY:	Well one entry suggested that Ms Lacox had hidden Ms Preston's pen. There was no evidence of this and it seemed pretty...silly really. I mean the notebook provided no real detail and there are boxes and boxes of pens in the stationary cupboard near every team. It was hard to believe that someone would bother to hide someone's pen as part of a process of harassment given that the actual inconvenience would have been minimal. If it had happened dozens of times that would have been different but as it was...
DEF:	Was that the only example of some of Ms Preston's allegations being...shall we say...*unlikely*?
KAY:	No they were on virtually every page - a mixture of things really - Instances where Ms Lacox hadn't held the lift for Ms Preston or declined to help her with a customer's call. Like I said, it was more a general lack of courtesy than anything else.
DEF:	From a professional point of view will you tell the court what your ultimate conclusion was in regards to this document?
KAY:	Well...
DEF:	In your own words is fine Ms Kay
KAY:	I concluded that Ms Preston was probably a bit...*unwell* mentally. I don't mean crazy or insane, but certainly...*eccentric* and possibly prone to paranoia. I also began to wonder if this state might be linked to her absenteeism.
DEF:	Meaning what?
KAY:	Well, often people who are facing a disciplinary procedure for absenteeism start to look at ways of excusing it or avoiding formal action. One of these might be to claim they were

absent through work related stress and blame their manager or employer. Another way might be to claim they are being bullied - the aim being that if the employer fears legal action or scandal they'll ignore the issue with the employee.

DEF: Does this strategy ever work?

KAY: In my experience it can do from time to time and it *is* becoming more prevalent.

DEF: Indeed. Regarding Ms Preston's complaint; what did you do next?

KAY: I suggested to Ms Preston that I would discuss the matter further with her line manager. It was my intention to do so the week that Mr King contacted myself in relation to the issue within his own team.

DEF: Now if we can return to Mr King's query. What did you suggest he did?

KAY: I advised that he separated them... Ms Lacox and Ms Preston. There was a vacancy in the invoicing department and I suggested that Ms Preston should be encouraged to a move as a development opportunity.

DEF: Wasn't that simply brushing the problem to one side?

KAY: Not really, the invoicing department was less pressurised and required people that were good with figures. It was a logical move for Ms Preston and had the advantage of separating two people who obviously didn't get on.

DEF: In fact a perfect solution all round?

KAY: That was my thought.

DEF: Did Ms Preston take the position?

KAY: She did not. Mr King made the suggestion to her and I believe she became upset. The following day she began a period of sickness absence from which, I believe, she has yet to return.

DEF: I see. I have no more questions M'lud.

(DEF sits PROS stands)

PROS: Just a few questions Ms Kay. Now you say you read Ms Preston's book in some detail?

KAY: Yes.

PROS: And found no case of harassment?

KAY: No

PROS: So if there was no evidence whatsoever of harassment why were they to be separated?

46

KAY: As I said, it was a logical solution.

PROS: But it wasn't from Ms Preston's point of view was it? In fact it made her considerably distressed?

KAY: Unfortunately yes, but once she had time to consider the opportunity she may well have seen it as a positive move.

PROS: Or she might, in fact, have seen it as somebody she had been asking for support playing right into her persecutor's hands?

KAY: That…hadn't occurred to me…

PROS: After 12 years working as a Human Resources consultant it didn't occur to you?

KAY: No.

PROS: Finally Ms Kay, you were going to issue Ms Preston a warning letter regarding her sickness absence levels?

KAY: Yes, that is correct.

PROS: Did Dunstons absentee policy discuss sickness with individuals? By this I mean, did Ms Preston's manager keep records as to why she was off sick? Her sickness notes from her GP? Did he note any patterns to yourselves in the HR department?

KAY: The absentee policy at Dunstons was more…generic.

PROS: Was support ever offered to anyone at Dunstons suffering from…say…a stress related absence?

KAY: No

PROS: Was any real enquiry ever made into the nature of frequent absenteeism by any individual employee at Dunstons?

KAY: Not as far as I know.

PROS: So Ms Preston may have been suffering from any number of conditions from…cancer to severe stress and all you would have done was totted up the days and instances and then issued the warning letter?

KAY: I'm afraid so.

PROS: So Ms Preston's absence COULD have had a direct link to what was going on within her team and your department would have known nothing about it?

KAY: That…is correct.

PROS: Ms Kay, you left Dunstons in March of this year. May I ask why?

KAY: Because… well… because I felt the processes Dunston's had in place didn't support Human Resources within their workforce or corporate planning. I felt my skills could be put to better use elsewhere.

PROS: I'm sure they can be. I have no further questions M'lud.

          (KAY leaves the stand)

Scene 3

(PROS sits, DEF stands)

DEF: I call Doctor Liam Foster.

(FOSTER enters and takes the stand)

FOSTER: I do swear and affirm that the evidence I give shall be the truth, the whole truth and nothing but the truth.

DEF: You are Doctor Liam Foster of Kings Down, Norwich?

FOSTER: I am.

DEF: And you are a practicing follower of the Legeesa faith?

FOSTER: Well I must correct you slightly there. Legeesa isn't a faith any more than any other belief system. To call it a faith would be to suggest that there is an element of... or lack of... proof in its abilities or its history. This isn't the case at all.

DEF: Well what would be a better way to describe it, so that the jury, and myself, might understand better?

FOSTER: Well Legeesa is a very old religion. One can trace its roots to Ireland way before any European influences. Essentially the word 'Legeesa' means healer in old Gaelic. I could talk all day about the history and ideas but... for the benefit of the jury... and yourself... one might imagine it as a healing religion which mixes certain elements of druidism, paganism, wiccan and even some oriental beliefs. In the same way as Christianity is a mish mash of a number of belief systems, so too is Legeesa. But it doesn't demand sacrifice, blind obedience or... faith. However, if you are more comfortable terming it in that way I shall endeavor to do so... for you and the court to better understand.

DEF: I see. So the principal at its core is one of healing?

FOSTER: Yes, that is correct.

DEF: Now you have some seniority in this religion do you not?

FOSTER: Well its hard to say. There is no real rank system. I have been practicing for some thirty years but Legeesa is not like a branch of Macdonalds - you don't gain seniority by passing exams or getting gold stars on a badge. Its simply experience that grants me any kind of... 'authority' as you might put it.

DEF: I see. So how might one become a follower or, I believe you call them, Legeesa Healers?

FOSTER: Well usually one is brought to it by friends. Some hear about it through books or the internet while others actually have been healed themselves and found the whole thing was something they wanted to be a part of.

DEF: So a practitioner of Legeesa, what might they be able to do? I mean in terms of this healing?

FOSTER: Well any number of things, they might be able to make medicines from herbs and other items. They might be able to help a patient relax and meditate in order to help them with things like stress or blood pressure. They may be able to apply certain teachings and disciplines to help a patient overcome things like cigarettes or alcohol. As with any ability to heal, if one studies enough the possibilities are virtually limitless.

DEF: Now my client, Miss Lacox, is a follower of this faith, this belief system. Do you know her personally?

FOSTER: I do. She has attended a number of 'gathering of friends' over the past few years. That is what we call our 'services'. We meet at certain dates in the old pagan calendar and talk, tell stories and work together to develop our own skills.

DEF: How skilled is Ms Lacox in the application of some of these healing techniques?

FOSTER: She is decidedly competent. She worked hard in her first years with us and I would say I would certainly trust her if I were sick or conflicted and found myself at her door.

DEF: So she applied herself to learning to become a Legeesa healer with some commitment then?

FOSTER: Most certainly.

DEF: Now I'm sure my learned friend will ask you the question but I'm going to save them the trouble. Can the teachings and practices of Legeesa be used to 'curse'?

FOSTER: No. Legeesa healers are no more witches and warlocks than jewish people are frugal with money or Muslims are terrorists. It is an argument that demeans the person making it far more than it damages Legeesa.

DEF: Are there any skills Ms Lacox might have learned from Legeesa that might have helped her harass Ms Preston in the ways that have been described in this court?

FOSTER: I would very much doubt it. Becoming involved in a healing belief in order to learn skills that might do harm is like learning to bake in order to poison somebody. There are easier ways to achieve your objective, and far less time consuming ones.

DEF: Dr Foster. You have heard that there was considerable animosity between Ms Lacox and Ms Preston. How would you, as a Legeesa practitioner view that?

FOSTER: We're all human. I don't particularly like my next door neighbor but that doesn't make me any less good at what I do as a healer.

DEF: Just a couple of final questions Dr Foster. Does Legeesa contain any teachings or doctrine which encourages its practitioners to deliberately cause harm?

FOSTER: Absolutely not.

DEF: Does it involve effigies like the one described as being left on Ms Preston's desk?

FOSTER: Oh dear me no.

DEF: And if a Legeesa healer was found to be trying to cause others harm what would be the position of the wider faith?

FOSTER: Such practices go against what we believe in very deeply. I would expect such a person to be expelled from the gatherings.

DEF: To your knowledge, has anyone, in the time you have been involved in Legeesa, ever been expelled or sanctioned for behaviour of this kind?

FOSTER: I have never heard of any such instances.

DEF: Thank you Dr Foster, No further questions.

            (DEF sits PROS stands)

PROS: Dr Foster, my learned colleague has already asked one of my questions so, with your permission, I'll try another. You stated earlier that as an example of Legeesa, one might learn the skill involved in giving up smoking is that correct?

FOSTER: Yes, that's right.

PROS: How would one do that?

FOSTER: Well the healer would ensure the patient was entirely relaxed, they would speak in a certain way and use certain phrases to lower the interest or belief the subject had in their addiction. They may give them certain verbal triggers which re-create this feeling of relaxation and freedom from addiction that the patient might use in their daily life. It would depend where the healers skills lie and the thoughts and feelings of the patient.

PROS: Is not another word for that Neuro-linguistic Programming?

FOSTER: What?

PROS: NLP Doctor, a technique practiced by hypnotherapists, psychotherapists, even stage performers. Hardly an ancient or original thing.

FOSTER: You may call it that. I believe the term is relatively new in science to describe a technique of simply communicating a message, a feeling or a state of mind. The discipline and work of a Legeesa healer is entirely open to both question and scrutiny. You must understand that this cynicism is something I have grown used to over the years, just as those of other beliefs face similar prejudice. It's hardly an act of evil to speak to someone in such a way that they leave the conversation thinking about things, or themselves differently. Teachers do it every day. As do barristers do they not?

PROS: So you will admit that Ms Lacox had a skill in NLP?

FOSTER: Its entirely possible.

PROS: Don't you know?

FOSTER: I'm not psychic. If she has read any of the old texts, or even the new ones - its possible. But it's the application of this leaning that is important. Ms Lacox is a member of a very old faith entirely based around healing, not *smiting* your enemies. Legeesa has existed for thousands of years. It has never been persecuted in the way that other religions have from pagans to christians. Why? Because we are healers. We ask for no money and require no reward. We have never sought power and pose no threat to kings, armies or emperors. And thus we have survived and continue to do so.

PROS: Indeed. Now finally Doctor Foster, you said there were any manner of ways in which someone may approach the Legeesa religion and become a part of it. May I ask if you have any criterea for joining?

FOSTER: Does any religion?

PROS: I would hope that one that teaches skills like NLP would. Well Doctor?

FOSTER: Not as such. But as I said, people who mean others harm are unlikely to join a religion of healers are they?

PROS: No criterea at all?

FOSTER: Apart from a willingness to learn and help others, no.

PROS: And so Ms Lacox, or anyone could just walk through the door?

FOSTER: As could you.

PROS: No further questions.

(FOSTER leaves the stand and takes his seat next to the dock in obvious support of LACOX)

Scene 4

(FOSTER leaves the stand. PROS sits, DEF stands)

DEF: I call the defendant, Ms Anouska Jayne Lacox

(LACOX walks from the dock to the witness stand)

LACOX: I do solemnly swear and affirm that the evidence I give shall be the truth, the whole truth and nothing but the truth.

DEF: You are Anouska Jayne Lacox

LACOX: That's right.

DEF: You live at 12 Allenby Terrace, Wantage

LACOX: Correct

DEF;   And you currently work at Dunstons Assurance in Milton?

LACOX: For the moment, yes.

DEF: For the moment?

LACOX: Well, I am currently suspended pending the outcome of this... trial.

DEF: Were you given a reason for this suspension?

LACOX: Yes, I was told that I would be suspended on full pay until the outcome was known and that I may face internal disciplinary action for bringing the company into disrepute.

DEF: Even in the event of an acquittal?

LACOX: That is what I was led to believe.

DEF: I see. Well... let us continue to discuss your employment at Dunstons for a moment if we may? How long have you worked there?

LACOX: About 4 years.

DEF: And your career – how has it progressed?

LACOX: I've not done too badly. I started as a clerical temp. I'm now deputy manager of the FE – that is, the Financial Enquiries team.

DEF: Do you enjoy your work?

LACOX: Actually I do, very much.

DEF: It's a high pressure position is it not?

LACOX:	I suppose it can be. I never really felt like that. I liked the fact that we were always busy, that there was always something to be striving for. It's not for everybody but... well... what job is? I liked the pressure... it gave the whole department a... buzz I suppose.
DEF:	Indeed... now Ms Preston came to work at Dunstons about 18 months after you, is that right?
LACOX:	I think that's about right.
DEF:	How was your working relationship with Ms Preston in the early days?
LACOX:	We got on ok. I mean we never went for a drink after work or even out to lunch or anything like that, but Ms Preston wasn't particularly social... well... that's not fair... some of the team socialised, others didn't... Ms Preston was one of those who didn't. I never held it against her but we only ever talked at work and mainly about work stuff.
DEF:	Now Both Ms Preston and Mr King, your former manager, have stated that the situation between yourself and Ms Preston deteriorated around October of last year.
LACOX:	That's right. It would have been the first weekend.
DEF:	And what was the reason for this?
LACOX:	Well... Alice... Ms Preston... tended to go sick quite a lot. Mainly during times when we were expected to be busy but also on other regular occasions... bank holiday's, nice days in the summer, that sort of thing. It was a bit of a running... well... *joke* isn't the right word but... well... everyone *knew* it. One of the team said she was off more times that John Wayne's safety catch... she tended to go sick at... I suppose you might call it *'convenient'* times? Convenient to her at least.
DEF:	And this was the case on this weekend?
LACOX:	Yes. It was the weekend of the wedding of one of my friends. It was up in Newcastle and we, my husband and I, were going up on the Friday during the day, go to the wedding on the Saturday and then come back on the Sunday. I had arranged to be off... everything was arranged.
DEF:	So what happened?
LACOX:	Alice called in sick on Thursday. She was rosta'd to work the Friday and Saturday. I was the reserve.
DEF:	The reserve?
LACOX:	The one who has to go in at the weekend if the person on the rota is ill. That way the team is always at full strength, even at weekends. Basically emergency sick cover.
DEF:	Surely with this wedding you could have swapped being the... reserve?

LACOX: I tried, the minute Anouska called in sick. Unfortunately everyone else had plans so I was stuck with it. She was sick again on the Friday so that was that. She was also off on the Saturday.

DEF: So you missed the wedding?

LACOX: I finished work at 3pm. By then it was too late to get all the way up there. So yes, I missed the wedding.

DEF: And Ms Preston returned to work on the Monday?

LACOX: As if she'd never been ill, smile on her face and fully recovered!

DEF: Were you angry with Ms Preston?

LACOX: Yes I was. I mean you don't just do that to people... not if they had plans. We were supposed to be a team. That gets messed up if someone lets down everyone else by always being sick. I'm surprised Mr King didn't mention that, it was practically an obsession for him!

PROS: Objection M'lud.

JUSTICE: Indeed. Mr Buell. I would ask that the defendant restrict herself to answering only the questions put to her. Please do so Ms Lacox. Stick to the facts and avoid adding your own embellishments and opinions if you please?

LACOX: Oh... ok... sorry my lord.

DEF: Apologies M'lud. (to LACOX) It is shortly after this Ms Preston then begins her lengthy document listing the perceived 'slights' and 'looks' that she alleges you began to give her. To illustrate by example. On 16 October you declined to assist her with a difficult customer on the telephone. What can you tell the court about this?

LACOX: Simple, if Alice wanted to go sick and inconvenience the rest of the team, and certainly me, I was not going to help her anymore. We all had a job to do, we all got the same pay more or less, but her 'sickies' had now started to affect me. I was just not willing to carry her anymore. She could deal with her own calls like the rest of us in the team had to.

DEF: I see. A little later in the month she notes you not making her a cup of coffee when you made one for others. Do you remember that?

LACOX: Well surely that's not a crime? If I accidently miss someone off the coffee list?

DEF: On 29 October she notes you *twice* failed to hold the lift for her. Do you recall these incidents?

LACOX: No, but it could have happened. I mean there are lifts at Dunstons, the doors close, sometimes people don't get to them in time... but to be fair, there are many lifts and do you know what? Miraculously they go up and down all the time! Is not holding a lift because I didn't see her coming a crime too? If so I suggest we build some more prisons!

JUSTICE:	Ms Lacox you have been warned.

LACOX: I'm sorry sir, it just....well...I'm sorry!

DEF: Now Ms Preston's diary is quite a long document. It contains numerous notes along these lines. How *would* you account for them?

LACOX: Well, I mean she was obviously imagining them. I mean I didn't like her I make no excuse for that. I tried to distance myself from her. I didn't want to be friendly because of the way she had screwed me over. If she felt unhappy about that well, I'm sorry...but I maintain the right to avoid someone I dislike. That's what I did. Work didn't suffer, I was still professional and good at my job. I even got promoted in spite of all the complaints Alice made. But you have the right surely, to stay away from people you don't like? Thankfully there's no law telling you who you have to be friends with!

DEF: So all the incidents in the office were just...minor attempts by you to avoid someone you had come to not care for?

LACOX: Yes. Not crimes, just simple...avoidances.

DEF: Now there are other incidents noted in this diary aside from incidents of simple avoidance. You are aware of that?

LACOX: Yes, the policeman told me. But they were all...well...twisted out of proportion.

DEF: Indeed, let us look at a few of these incidents in more detail. On November 15th it was noted that Ms Preston went to the lavatories. After a short time you were sent to see if there was anything the matter is that right?

LACOX: More or less.

DEF: More or less?

LACOX: Mr King said something like 'where the hell is she? Go and track her down will you?'

DEF: I see, and did you?

LACOX: Yes, the toilets is a pretty obvious place to look. Its where Alice tended to go when she was...upset...or doing a disappearing act.

DEF: In fact, the cause of her distress on this occasion was because her plant had died is that not so?

LACOX: I believe so. She didn't tell me directly. I found her in the loo, I told her King was looking for her and she'd better pull herself together. That was about it. I had work to do and...as you said yourself...I had tracked her down as requested.

DEF: So when did you find out about the reason for her distress?

LACOX:	I was heading for lunch and King caught up with me in the corridor. He said something like 'You haven't killed her plant have you?' I was a bit surprised at this and asked him what he meant. He told me that Alice had a plant she was fond of on the desk and it had died...or been deliberately killed. He asked me if I had done it.
DEF:	And had you?
LACOX:	Don't be ridiculous. Of course not. I mean...what sort of a question is that? Am I on trial for being a danger to horticulture now too?
JUSTICE:	Ms Lacox I would advise you to restrict yourself to answering the questions put to you by council.
LACOX:	I'm sorry your worship but this is what this is all about. I'm being accused of not being sympathetic to a...raving lunatic and for causing her to attempt suicide by a complicated plot involving 'looks' and plant murder! Is this really what our court system is for? Is all the money this has cost being spent correctly?.. *Really?*
JUSTICE:	I have heard quite enough. Ms Lacox this court is not your personal platform. You will restrict yourself to answering council's questions or I warn you there will be consequences is that understood?
LACOX:	I'm...sorry your worship...I'm also sorry that I called Alice a...well...what I did. It wasn't fair and it wasn't right. Please accept my apologies.
JUSTICE:	Very well. But I shan't tell you again. Proceed Mr Buell
DEF:	Now in her...*document* and in evidence she has presented here, Ms Preston lists an occasion on 10 February when you 'followed' her home on the bus she usually used. Did you actually take this bus?
LACOX:	Well this is the thing. I *did* take the bus...the 4C. And it's quite right that I usually drive but my car was off the road. In fact that's *why* I took the 4C – which *is* completely the wrong one. I should have got on the 4X which would have got me home in about 20 minutes but I didn't know because I never use busses. The 4C went to every village from Milton to Didcot, to East Hendred, Ardington and finally Wantage. It took me an hour and a half but the fact is that I never use the busses. I saw what I thought was the right one...it had a '4' written on it...and just got on.
DEF:	So you had no idea Ms Lacox was to take the bus too?
LACOX:	No
DEF:	When you were on the bus did you *stare* at her?
LACOX:	No
DEF:	When you were on the bus did you make *any* attempt to intimidate her?
LACOX:	No. I sat down and that was it.

DEF:	Did you see Ms Preston get off the bus?
LACOX:	No. Once I realised I was on the wrong bus I got a book out and started reading, that or mucking about with my phone. I have no idea when she got off.
DEF:	So it was a simple coincidence?
LACOX:	Yes.
DEF:	Did you ever take this or any other bus home from Dunstons again?
LACOX:	No. My car was repaired the following day and I haven't had to get the bus since.
DEF:	Now the most significant incident as noted in Ms Preston's diary occurred on the 16th. On this night, she states, she woke up at about 3am, went to her bedroom window and saw you standing in her front garden staring up at her house.
LACOX:	Well I mean that's utterly ridiculous. I didn't even know where she lived. What would I have to gain by doing that other than catching pneumonia?
DEF:	You were never there?
LACOX:	No
DEF:	Now on 20 February you were invited to Abingdon Police station by Constable Jelkes to discuss the situation between yourself and Ms Preston. It was here that you were invited to give your side of the story?
LACOX:	That's not quite right. I was basically ordered to the station under what I assumed to be the threat of arrest. When a police call you out of the blue and 'invite' you to come in 'for a chat about a very serious incident' you do as you're told don't you?
DEF:	Now when Constable Jelkes addressed the situation and told you that he was concerned that the situation between yourself and Ms Preston had got out of hand?
LACOX:	No, he implied that my actions had caused Ms Preston to attempt suicide, or at least to harm herself. He suggested, with no subtlety at all, that I was responsible and had deliberately done so.
DEF:	And what was your reaction?
LACOX:	Well... I...
DEF:	Please answer the question Ms Lacox
LACOX:	To be honest I told him to sod off.
DEF:	Why did you do that?

LACOX:	Well look at it from my position. I was having my dinner with my husband and all of a sudden the telephone goes. 'Hello – police here. Best you get yourself down to the station to answer some questions!' so there I am. From no cares in the world to fretting about what the hell I might have done in a matter of seconds. I get to the station and all of a sudden this police officer is sitting me in an interview room and making some pretty unpleasant insinuations. And why? Because I had had an argument with someone at work! It was that simple – a silly argument – one that even my manager wasn't bothered with – and all of a sudden I'm under suspicion of a criminal act! I just…well I just thought 'who the hell are they – to accuse me?' That they could take me out of my nice home…my nice life…and suddenly suggest that I was a…*criminal*…I mean I could have lost my job, my *home*! All because of the ramblings of some woman in a bloody diary!
DEF:	So you refused to co-operate?
LACOX:	Yes I did! The more I thought about it the more angry I got. I mean this was all down to me and Alice not getting on…well surely you have the right not to get on with someone? Surely you can dislike someone without ending up at the police station…or even in court? That's what this is all about. Me and Alice didn't get on. So Alice, who isn't a well woman, started keeping a diary of her own imaginings, and then hurt herself. All of a sudden I'm getting a call and some oaf of a copper is accusing me of harassment and telling me how much trouble I could get in! Well sod him! Sod them both!
DEF:	Ms Lacox, I appreciate you are upset but I might suggest you take a breath for a moment?
JUSTICE:	That is good advice Mr Buell
DEF:	Now…Your not answering Constable Jelkes questions…Do you regret this now?
LACOX:	Partly…but the point remains…it was an argument at work between colleagues…it was playground stuff…at best…and now one of us is in the dock! I mean what sort of country do we *really* live in?
DEF:	So, to be clear, Ms Lacox, have you *ever* deliberately tried to intimidate Ms Preston either at work or anywhere else?
LACOX:	Absolutely not. I have better things to do!
DEF:	Have you ever visited Ms Preston's house for any other reason?
LACOX:	No

(PROS begins writing deliberately)

DEF:	Have you called Ms Preston's telephone?
LACOX:	No
DEF:	Have you ever knocked on her front door?
LACOX:	No

DEF:	Have you left effigies on her desk?
LACOX:	No
DEF:	Have you deliberately tried to make her work life difficult?
LACOX:	No
DEF:	Do you bear Ms Preston *any* ill will?
LACOX:	Well...I will be honest...I don't *like* her. I never pretended otherwise but look where that has got me! But I mean her no harm, and I never have. She's...sad...Ill...sick.
DEF:	No further questions.

(DEF sits PROS rises)

PROS:	Ms Lacox is it fair to say that for most of the time you were at Dunstons you worked closely with Ms Preston?
LACOX:	We were on the same team, she sat opposite me on the bank of desks we used.
PROS:	So you were in close proximity to her most of the time?
LACOX:	I suppose so, if you want to put it like that.
PROS:	Were you aware if or when she was upset about anything?
LACOX:	Well...yes and no...she tended to get upset about...well...*things*. By that I mean work stuff. If her bus was late she'd be very flustered. If she had a difficult customer, if the computer system froze, if the printer jammed, if she lost a pen...virtually anything could set her off at any time...Alice crying at work was by no means unusual.
PROS:	But you had no idea that you were the direct cause of ...'setting her off'?
DEF:	M'lud I object.
JUSTICE:	Quite right too. You know better than that Ms D'Marco
PROS:	Apologies M'lud. Ms Lacox, did you have any idea why Ms Preston was so upset on 9 January?
LACOX:	What happened then?
PROS:	It was the day you were asked by Mr King to go and see where Ms Preston was after he had noticed she was absent from her desk.
LACOX:	Oh I see. No, not at the time.
PROS:	When then?

LACOX: The following morning probably. Some of the team were talking about the fact that some sort of voodoo doll had been put on her desk. One of them even asked if I had cast a spell on her.

PROS: And what was your reaction to this?

LACOX; I think I probably found it rather funny.

PROS: The joke against Ms Preston?

LACOX: No... the link between Legeesa and voodoo. It took a certain level of stupidity to make that connection. Or to suggest that I could actually cast *spells*. As I remember I didn't give Ms Preston's reaction any thought but the ignorance of my workmates was quite amusing. It tended to happen a lot and you sort of got used to it.

PROS: So you didn't leave the effigy on her desk?

LACOX; No. It's ridiculous.

PROS: But you had played up to the... *mythology*... within the team that you were some kind of a witch?

LACOX: Well... it *was* pretty funny... because it was so far from the truth... it was like a caricature. It was no more true than suggesting that you are a pantomime dame just because you are wearing a wig.

PROS: Indeed. And you never noticed the effect it was having on Ms Preston?

LACOX: No.

PROS: Even though she sat opposite you?

LACOX: *No.*

PROS: Let's move onto the more serious incidents covered in Ms Preston's diary - The bus journey that occurred on 10 February. Now you stated that you had no idea Ms Lacox was to take the bus on that day?

LACOX: No, how could I?

PROS: How about when you stood together at the bus stop?

LACOX: Oh I see. Well no... I didn't see her at the bus stop. I was running late and jumped on the bus just as it was about to pull away. Ms Preston was already onboard.

PROS: Did you see the bus arrive?

LACOX: No

PROS: When you got on did you see Ms Preston?

LACOX:	Yes.
PROS:	Where was Ms Preston sitting?
LACOX:	Umm…by the window I think. About half way down.
PROS:	On which side?
LACOX:	The side…well, I'm not sure if you call it the left or the right…the side *not* behind the driver.
PROS:	The side closest to the kerb if the bus was facing towards the Didcot end of Milton Park?
LACOX:	Yes, that's right.
PROS:	From which direction did you approach the bus?
LACOX:	From the front door of Dunstons. The bus stop is at the bottom of the path.
PROS:	So you approached the bus from the side?
LACOX:	Yes.
PROS:	So how did you know it was a number 4 bus?
LACOX:	I'm sorry?
PROS:	You stated that you didn't see the bus arrive. The number of the bus is written on the front and rear yet you approached it from the side. How did you know that it was the right bus to take?
LACOX:	Well…it wasn't the right bus to take was it?
PROS:	How did you know it was even a number 4 bus?
LACOX:	Well…I…I suppose someone must have told me that the busses that left from that stop were the number 4's. I can't really remember.
PROS:	You can't really remember?
LACOX:	Well I didn't know at the time that an innocent bus journey would be so important.
PROS:	I put it to you that you saw Ms Preston get on the bus. You could even see where she was sitting. This was when you decided to get on as well. You knew the bus would get you home eventually and so why not take a longer route home to torment your victim? That's what happened isn't it?
LACOX:	No it was a simple…and quite innocent, *mistake*!
PROS:	Have you told the truth today Ms Lacox?

LACOX:	I...I think so.
PROS:	What about visiting Ms Preston's house. You stated that you had never been there is that not so?
LACOX:	That's right.
PROS:	How long have you lived in Wantage?
LACOX:	About 12 months or so
PROS:	Where did you live before then?
LACOX:	Harwell.
PROS:	A number of the team lived in Harwell, Didcot, Milton at the time did they not?
LACOX:	Yes
PROS:	And you shared lifts to work?
LACOX:	In the early days yes. For a short time before I moved.
PROS:	How many of you
LACOX:	Four, sometimes five depending on rotas.
PROS:	Including Ms Preston?
LACOX:	Occasionally.
PROS:	So occasionally you were in a car when Ms Preston was picked up or dropped off at her home?
LACOX:	Well...I mean I never really paid any attention. It would have been months ago and I scarcely remembered it.
PROS:	But it *did* happen?
LACOX:	Well...perhaps once or twice...ages ago. But to be honest I had forgotten.
PROS:	You had forgotten?
LACOX:	Visiting some street or another over 18 months ago for a few seconds? Yes *I had forgotten!*
PROS:	But you remember now don't you? Now finally I would like to ask you about your opinion of Ms Preston. You stated that you thought she was Ill. Is that all?
LACOX:	What do you mean?
PROS:	You don't hold her responsible for your current predicament?

LACOX: Well... I don't know.

PROS: Come now Ms Lacox, by your own words this was an office argument that has led to a criminal trial? The whole thing has caused you considerable time, trouble and expense. It has put your reputation, your professional career and even potentially your liberty at risk. Are you seriously telling me that you bear Ms Preston no ill will?

LACOX: I DO NOT.

PROS: But she has directly accused you and no-one else. If you are entirely innocent then this situation is ALL Ms Preston's fault. Aren't you the slightest bit angry?

DEF: M'lud, is this really a question that will help us find the truth?

LACOX: Of course I'm angry! And I told you already I don't like Ms Preston. I think she's a... a sick and twisted individual!

PROS: Your contention is that she *is* in some way ill?

LACOX: Yes it bloody well is!

DEF: M'lud?

JUSTICE: I would ask council for the prosecution to get to the point.

PROS: Then I have only one more question M'lud. Ms Lacox. If you have dedicated so much of your time to working to help others. By learning skills, by reading books, by attending meetings, and you genuinely wanted to be a *healer*... why didn't you try to help Ms Preston? If you were so convinced of her... illness... why didn't you make a single offer to help *her*? If everything you believe and live by is based on helping others... why didn't *you* reach out to *her*?

LACOX: Well because... well she probably wouldn't have...

PROS: Because she made you miss a *wedding*... and you *hated* her for it! I think as a reflection of your character everything is now much clearer. Thank you Ms Lacox, I have no further questions.

JUSTICE: You may return to the dock Ms Lacox.

          (LACOX returns to the dock where a GUARD now stands in anticipation of the verdict)

DEF: The defence rests M'lud.

JUSTICE: Would council care to commence summing up?

          (PROS rises)

PROS: Ladies and Gentlemen of the jury. I told you at the beginning of this trial that this isn't a case of witchcraft. In fact its a simple and sad case of the harassment of a weaker person by a stronger one. It's no different to the unpleasant practice of 'trolling' on the internet, or the kind of playground bullying that many of us may have seen or even experienced when we were at school. It is also no less criminal. In all cases like these its about how the victim was made to feel. A joke on the internet meant to amuse that causes offence *can* be seen legally as harassment. Likewise any action which obviously intimidates: - stealing a stapler, following someone home, knocking over a coffee cup. So small and insignificant that their seriousness is ignored – until its too late.

Now we've seen how Ms Lacox had studied and learned certain skills which would make her a potentially very dangerous enemy - particularly to a vulnerable woman like Ms Preston. We've seen how she employed these skills over a period of time to devastating effect. We have seen how Ms Preston's health has deteriorated, we have seen how her professional career has suffered, we have seen how Ms Lacox successfully persecuted Ms Preston, her enemy, while continuing to rise in her own professional life, and we have seen that the only real defence offered in this court by Ms Lacox has been a simple and haughty denial.

Part of the skill Ms Lacox employed to achieve her names lie in the subtlety of the whole enterprise. But it wasn't so subtle that it was unnoticed by Ms Preston's manager at work. It wasn't so subtle it was unnoticed by her doctor. It wasn't so subtle it was ignored by the police and, most importantly, it wasn't so subtle that it wasn't noticed by Ms Preston.

But then, that was the idea wasn't it?

You all heard Ms Preston give evidence. Did she come across as neurotic? Did she come across as mentally ill? Or was she just plain scared? Was she exhausted? Was she worn out? Harassment of the kind experienced by the victim *is* exhausting but Ms Preston was still able to confront her persecutor. Was her testimony confused? - No, absolutely not. In spite of *everything* Ms Preston was able to name her tormentor, and explain precisely had had been perpetrated against her during this nightmare, for make no mistake – this was a nightmare for Ms Preston. A nightmare she sought to free herself from by taking the only instrument to hand and attempting to end her own life rather than continue to endure it. Now there is another way to end this nightmare. *You* can end it. By finding the defendant – guilty.

(PROS sits DEF rises)

DEF: I'm going to do something very unusual now - I'm going to ask you to put yourself in the position of the victim. Imagine that you had been suffering from anxiety and possibly depression that has, over the last year, become steadily more debilitating. Perhaps you fear the diagnosis of a mental health issue and the stigma that might go with it, perhaps you fear becoming dependent on medication. Valiantly, you try to fight it yourself. You take the occasional time off work and try as best you can to cope without the intrusion of others. Unfortunately, this is a cruel condition that doesn't respond and steadily, almost without noticing, you become more fearful of the world around you. Everything is a threat, everything is something to be terrified of - young people in the street, fireworks, an up-turned dustbin…and somebody at work with whom you have had an argument. Imagination is a wonderful thing but when linked with an untreated mental health condition it can be dangerous. It can be horrific. We've seen the effects of that mixture in this very court.

65

With this in mind I ask you to put yourself in victim's position when the light went out. Was it a simple and small electrical problem? Or something more dangerous? An earthquake? A terrorist attack? ... *Witchcraft?* Without rationality anything can be intimidating, and it *was* only Ms Preston who screamed when the lights went out wasn't it?

Now I'd like you to put yourself in the position of the accused. An argument at work has led to a criminal investigation, questioning, arrest and ultimately... this trial. How would you react? Indignance? Astonishment? Anger? Are Ms Lacox reactions and refusal to show sympathy or remorse really *that* surprising?

Still in the position of the accused I would like you to ask one question; why would she *bother?* Ms Preston was no threat either personally or professionally to Ms Lacox and yet the prosecution would have you believe that the defendant carried through a plan to rob Ms Preston of her health and her sanity because she ruined a weekend away. Does that seem likely? Does it seem likely she would waste her time, energy and effort to pursue Ms Preston? To follow her home? To go out in the middle of the night into a howling gale just to stand in her garden and intimidate her? *Really?*

All the prosecution has offered in terms of evidence is speculation and they have offered *nothing* in terms of motive. All they have really offered at all is a victim – and Ms Preston is certainly that. But she is not a victim of Anouska Lacox, she is not a victim of harassment and she is not a victim of a curse. She is a victim of her own health and her own mental state. Its tragic but it is not the fault of Ms Lacox and so I would ask you to return a verdict of Not Guilty

JUSTICE: Members of the jury. It is time for you to briefly consider your verdict. This has been an emotional case and it might be easy to approach it from an emotional perspective. However, I must council you to weigh the evidence on the facts presented.

As to the charge; the law states that a person is guilty of aggravated criminal harassment if their actions *directly* contributed to the physical harm or injury of the victim. This includes the action of self-harm. If you believe that Ms Lacox actions forced or significantly influenced Ms Preston's actions on 18 February then you must return a verdict of guilty.

Alternatively, if you believe that there were other *significant* influences on Ms Preston's actions, whatever they may be, you must return a verdict of not guilty.

The clerk of the court will now advise you further.

(CLERK rises and addresses the audience)

CLERK: Ladies and Gentlemen of the jury would those of you who find the defendant guilty please raise your hands?

Would those of you who find the defendant not guilty please raise your hands?

Thank you.

JUSTICE: Defendant will rise.

(LACOX stands)

JUSTICE: **(Guilty)** Anouska Lacox you have been found guilty of Aggravated Criminal Harassment contrary to the 1998 Offences Against the Person Act. The actions you have taken have directly affected the physical and mental wellbeing of someone who you took a malignant and venomous dislike to. It is only by pure lucky chance that Ms Preston did not cause herself serious harm on 18 February and I am mindful that the events you deliberately set in motion may have had an even more tragic ending. I will waste no time in condemning you further as I fear it would fall upon deaf ears. Instead I intend to give you time to consider your actions... and what they have cost both your victim and yourself. I hereby sentence you to be imprisoned for 14 Months. Take her down.

(LACOX is removed from the courtroom)

JUSTICE: **(Not Guilty)** Anouska Lacox you have been found not guilty and are free to go.

(LACOX leaves the dock, pausing to look briefly at the now sobbing PRESTON, she leaves the court)

JUSTICE: Thank you for your time members of the jury. You are hereby discharged from your responsibilities and may I wish you a safe journey home?

End.

Thou Shalt Not Suffer - Programme Notes

Crown Court

I have always loved courtroom dramas. I find that the static nature of the setting lends itself very well to generating great performances and, because they inevitability tackle issues which appeal to our own personal sense of justice, they tend to create a wider debate which lingers long after the curtain falls or the credits roll.

I first came into contact with this kind of drama when I was a child with the tv series Crown Court. Crown Court began in the early 1970s and ran for fourteen years (effectively my entire childhood). It boasted casts which were a 'who's who' of highly respected actors (or those who eventually would be) including Patrick Troughton, Brian Cox and Alison Steadman. Furthermore, it was written by some of the best and most respected writers in the industry such as David Fisher, John Godber and Jeremy Sandford.

The premise was simple. Over three half-hour episodes (usually screened from Wednesday to Friday), a fictional case was presented before a judge and jury. The jury was made up of members of the public, and the verdict they reached on Friday afternoon was completely unscripted.

Screened at lunchtimes it was a favourite of non-working mums and sickly school kids alike due to its mix of decidedly adult themes (which over the years included child abuse, mental illness and murder), but also the high standard of story and performances. Because of this, in the days before video recorders, a child off sick from school and captivated by the first episode of a story often had to spin a 24 hour bug out to 3 days so that they could be at home to see the verdict.

For some of us – Crown Court, with its delivery of high quality drama in an extremely unlikely time slot, is as much a part of our memories of the weekday lunchtimes of our childhoods as the adverts for 'Don Amos – King of Caravans'. It is to the memory of this excellent series that Thou Shalt Not Suffer is respectfully dedicated.

'Thou Shalt Not Suffer'

Its hard to tell where I first came up with the premise of 'Thou Shalt Not Suffer'. Certainly I have wanted to write a courtroom drama for some time and this enthusiasm was certainly fuelled by my own experience of jury service a few years ago. As far as I can remember though, it all began in earnest with a conversation between myself and a friend over a Friday night beer, the traditional time to complain about work stuff.

My friend was a manager in a local business and had been required to put an accusation of bullying to one of his team members after a complaint had been made against them. Before the meeting he had looked into his company's 'Bullying and Harassment' policy and had been concerned that the

emphasis was not necessarily about the facts of the situation or what was said – but more about how the alleged victim was made to feel. This was the root of his dilemma as he was now required to proceed as dictated by some very inflexible rules and something as abstract as 'hurt feelings' This, he contended, could effectively be caused by anything depending on the person. Eventually we decided that HR policy should include the option of pistols at dawn- style duelling as it involved significantly less paperwork for managers however, it was my friend's initial dilemma which interested me and formed the central basis for the story – albeit with the stakes considerably raised.

I then set about writing it as a legal case. No easy task as it was imperative that the audience actually had points to consider as they watched the drama unfold. Even as I was tapping away at my laptop I tried to stifle any feelings of pity for either the alleged victim or perpetrator. I tried to keep the evidence balanced and weigh the scales of fictional justice evenly in terms of evidence and witness credibility. It was because of this effort that I was extremely nervous when we read the play through at the club in the summer of last year. The members read the play and, as with the audience tonight, were then to give a verdict by show of hands. If it was overwhelmingly one way or another I had failed. Thankfully it wasn't – the club was roughly split down the middle. The verdict you give tonight may well be different to that which the club gave or which will be given by the audience who sees this play tomorrow.

Because of this uncertainty it is actually a little difficult to explain in simple terms what this play is actually about. Simply put – if the audience finds Ms Lacox guilty it is about harassment – if they acquit her – it is about paranoia. As to whether justice is served – that's entirely up to you. Because of the way I had to write it even I, the author, don't know exactly if the defendant is innocent or guilty. I hope you enjoy trying to decide for yourselves.

'Thou Shalt Not Suffer' was first performed by Abingdon Drama Club at the Unicorn Theatre, Abingdon 21st – 24th June 2017.